WOMAN OF THE AVALON

WOMAN
of the
AVALON

L. L. Foreman

SAGEBRUSH
Large Print Westerns

First published in Great Britain by ISIS Publishing Ltd.
First published in the United States by Dell Books

Published in Large Print 2006 by ISIS Publishing Ltd.,
7 Centremead, Osney Mead, Oxford OX2 0ES
United Kingdom
by arrangement with
Golden West Literary Agency

British Library Cataloguing in Publication Data
Foreman, L. L. (Leonard London), 1901–
   Woman of the Avalon. – Large print ed. –
   (Sagebrush western series)
   1. Western stories
   2. Large type books
   I. Title
   813.5'2 [F]

ISBN-10 0–7531–7555–X (hb)
ISBN-13 978-0-7531-7555-2 (hb)

Printed and bound in Great Britain by
T. J. International Ltd., Padstow, Cornwall

CHAPTER
ONE

Od Thornton turned in, off the main trail, which ran past the east edge of town, and reined the hired buckboard team down to a sedate walk so as not to raise any more dust than necessary along the main street. Two trail outfits were camped this side of the Red when he crossed, and he guessed the storekeepers had enough to cuss about, the way those wild riders always roared into town, stamping up dust that billowed through the open doors and spread all over the merchandise.

Driving by the glaring white front of the Silver Palace, he saw Jim Bloud, one of its two owners, standing in the shade of the doorway smoking his morning cigar. Jim Bloud snatched the cigar from his mouth and his heavy red face flared a wary belligerence. Od Thornton returned him a poker look, and passed on.

It was too bad, he thought, that he had ever let that pair of Jims — Jim Bloud and Jim Kerry — into the town. A little business competition was all right, but the Silver Palace notoriously provided a lot more than that. He wondered at that look Bloud had sent him. The Jims had him about broken, as everybody knew, and

1

could afford to grin rather than glare. Maybe they had hoped he was gone for good.

In his tiny office farther along the street Heze Johns, the town marshal, raised his head at the sound of the buckboard and team. Heze had a colorless round face and eyes that never seemed quite to focus on anything. With a finger he marked his place on his newspaper, and then took off his reading glasses. Through his window he sent Od a nod that was curiously slow and reserved. Od nodded back.

For years they had built up a friendship, of a kind, and today this was all it amounted to: a bare nod of recognition. Well, that was how it went in this town, these bad days, when a man slipped down. Few would stand out square and side with the loser, especially if he had once been on top. There was more than a little satisfaction in seeing the big man go down.

Pulling in at the livery, Od said, "Morning, Ted," to young Ted Sieker who came out to take over the rig.

Because of Heze Johns's constrained manner, Od gave some attention to the young stableman's reaction, for he liked Ted.

"Morning, Od," Ted said, inspecting the team with needless care and not looking at him.

His trip, Od thought wryly, had turned up some value, after all. It was wise to get away for a spell. You came back noticing things — signs and attitudes that had changed so gradually you'd hardly been conscious of them before.

That seemed to be all from Ted, but Od waited, so Ted said, "Didn't look for you back this early."

Od flipped him a dollar and crossed the street to the Avalon. He wondered, with cold humor, what desperate purposes folks ascribed to his trip to Fort Griffin. Funny how they acted when they knew a man was hitting bottom.

He palmed open the swing doors of the Avalon, and as usual swept a fast inspection over the barroom. He liked to keep the Avalon clean and decent at all times. He had kept it so right through the raw days, not long ago, when the Avalon was the only real saloon worth mentioning between Fort Griffin and Trinidad on this off-shoot of the Chisholm Trail. In those days the trail hands satisfied their thirsts, took a whirl at the gambling tables, and left on time to push the herds north. With heavy heads, maybe, and light pockets, but good feelings all around. There had been no Silver Palace then.

This time Od's eyes, newly noticing, told him that the Avalon was cheerlessly clean. And deserted. The long bar gleamed with the well-rubbed luster of rich red mahogany, even in the dents and scars left by exuberant gun butts and high-kicked spurs. On the back-bar shelves the bottles and glasses rose in crystal tiers. The sanded barroom floor lay as immaculate as the tide-washed beach of an uninhabited island. No customers to mar it.

In the gambling room, reached by simply walking through a broad archway on the right of the barroom, the dust cloths had not been removed from the tables. The dance hall, at the left of the barroom and also

3

available through an archway, was a cavern, darkened and dismal, its empty floor reflecting eerily a pale streak of light from the barroom. The whole place was a spotless tomb. If somebody banged the piano, Od reflected, ghosts would rattle bones and point toward the Silver Palace — to the naked women and cat-eyed gamblers and sharpshooters and whisky with the hair on.

A lone bartender stood flatfooted on useless duty, waiting for a customer. His name was George and he was elderly and unhappy.

One man only sat at a table in the barroom, playing solitaire. He was Soft Duval, one of the last two Avalon house gamblers who hung on because Od still staked them to grub and they were fourth-rate and couldn't make up their minds where else to go.

Od said, "Morning, George. Morning, Soft."

George selected a glass and bottle. The Avalon still had plenty of stock. He filled the glass, a double shot. He turned to the back-bar shelf where he kept coffee hot on a spirit stove. He filled a white mug with black coffee and set it beside the whisky glass.

"You're back early," he commented. "Musta drove all night."

"Cooler at night." Od sipped coffee interspersed with bourbon, and made them come out even. "Fort Griffin's no good. Nobody there I could use here." He lighted a cigar, feeling better. It occurred to him that Soft Duval, at the table, hadn't uttered a word of greeting.

4

Edgy because of Heze Johns and Ted Sieker, Od asked Soft Duval curtly, "How's it go with you and the Duke?"

Soft Duval turned a card and scanned his layout. "The Duke's sick."

"How sick?"

The Duke's drinking habits occasionally caught up with him and laid him low. But his handling of cards amounted to art, and he was the only man in the Texas Panhandle who could sport a monocle and get away with it. The Duke and Soft Duval had been partners for three years.

"Bad sick," Soft Duval said. He furrowed his fingers through the solitaire layout, smearing it. "Last night the Duke drifted over to the Silver Palace. No — he wasn't quitting. Things were too dead here, that's all. The Duke went out to see could he steer a little trade here for the good o' the house."

"A sorry come-down," Od said. "For the Duke. For the house, too. He didn't make out?"

Soft Duval bunched the cards neatly. "We picked him up in Tolliver's wagon yard early's morning, George and me and young Sieker. He didn't get there by himself — as you'll know when you see him."

Od stepped away from the bar and paused at Soft's table. He was nearing thirty and had learned to harness hot impulses, but he never could quite match the cold impassiveness of Soft Duval and his kind. Soft raised his eyes; his look climbing leisurely up Od's black coat, lingering an instant at the glimpse of gun-belt and then at the diamond in the white linen shirt, and halting at Od's face.

"I'll see the Duke," Od said, and Soft got up and followed him out. George washed the empty glass and coffee mug, shaking his head slowly.

The Avalon's past progress could be traced through its architecture. Starting as a rowdy roadhouse on the new cattle trail, it sobered to the dignity of a stage stop and hotel when the South Plains Mail Line came through. The hotel part grew up as a string of rooms poking out from the rear, with a gallery. The gambling room and the dance hall got built on later, while the town was springing up all around to become a supply center for trail drivers and a depot for freighters.

Influenced by a profit-minded proprietor, the dance hall became the supply center for the rooms out back. The rooms lost their original purpose, the Avalon gained a certain name, and weary travelers sought their rest elsewhere.

After Od Thornton acquired the Avalon in forty straight hours of stud poker, he restored it to the proper balance. The gambling room had its rightful place, and those who wanted to dance were welcome. He put in new floors, mirrors, and bar equipment. He had little interest in running a hotel, and none in the other thing, so he turned the rooms over to the use of his hired staff — including a new bevy of dance-hall girls.

How they used their rooms, he told the girls, was their own concern. He only stipulated that they keep their activities private and unprofessional and within reasonable bounds of propriety. They did, on the whole, and for three years hardly any serious trouble marred the record of the flourishing Avalon — a solidly decent gambling-saloon, for male trade. The spangled Lulus weren't allowed at the bar; tables were set aside for them and their friends, served by a waiter in a white jacket. They weren't expected to raise their voices, either, but to behave as ladies and not bother the gambling men and earnest drinkers unless invited. All in all, an admirable house.

Its ruin set in with the rise of the Silver Palace. Into their gaudy establishment the Jims put every known honkytonk feature and a few of their own invention, including a brightly lighted stage, strip performers, cribs, spiked cider in champagne bottles, short-change experts, and something they called a girl lottery. They took the trade.

In the Duke's room Od gazed down at the shape in the bed. "He didn't snore like this before, did he?" he asked. Only a part of the Duke's face was visible between bandages, and that had the look of a clumsily skinned cow-carcass.

"Nose smashed," Soft Duval said quietly. He motioned to a coat hung on a chair. The seams were split open at the armpits. "Couple of 'em held him. Broke both his arms. Somebody else — Jim Bloud, I'd say — worked on him."

"Guess the Jims figured this would finally convince me I was through in Trailtown. They also, apparently, enjoyed their work."

The Duke snored on, bubbles of bloody mucus ballooning and bursting at his nostrils.

"Doc Moran says they musta put the boots to him after they drug him to the wagon yard," Soft mentioned. "I guess by then the Duke didn't feel it, though. Doc's with Emma May, if you want to see him."

Od said, "What?" Emma May was the Duke's girl. She was one of the few Lulus who still stuck to the Avalon. The others — even Gloria, the Avalon queen with the gold tiara bought by Od — had deserted to the Silver Palace.

Soft said understandingly, "No, not that. She went looking for the Duke when he didn't come back. Jim Bloud caught her. Or some of his bunch did. They was all over town last night — we shut down an' laid low. He broke her jaw. She came crawling to the back. But she ain't in this fix, anywhere near." Soft inclined his head at the snoring shape on the bed. "They sure done a job on him, eh?"

Od said, "I guess this is the day."

Soft spread his fingers and looked down at them. They were good fingers, still supple, although thickening at the joints. He was getting old; the blue veins and brown splotches said so. "They don't expect you back till tonight," he murmured.

"Jim Bloud saw me coming in."

"Oh." Soft closed his fingers. "They'll be ready, then. Not like they'd be tonight, but —"

He didn't finish, because Od ducked out through the door and his boots raised creakings along the gallery

8

floorboards. After another glance at the broken hulk on the bed, Soft left, quietly closing the door.

Walking into the barroom, Od shed his coat and as he threw it on the bar he saw himself in a back-bar mirror — white shirt, diamond, dark face, belt and gun bared at his waist. It came to him that quite some time had gone by since last he readied like this. He could be rusty.

That made a bad thought to take along into a fight. He threw it off, but noticed old George observing him searchingly. Some day, Od supposed, even old George would hang up his apron and quit him like the rest, unless something drastic was done to save the Avalon. No point in going down all the way to the bottom with a sinking ship after the rats left. No benefit in that for anybody.

Using both hands, Od hoisted his belt and slid it an inch, working the holstered gun into the precise hang suited to his right hand and length of arm. He struck the butt lightly with his palm, just once; it satisfied his habit of deliberation, while his cold rage said to hell with such preliminaries.

George untied his apron and laid it beside the coat. He plucked his black derby hat from under the bar and put it on, a sure sign that he intended venturing out into the light of day. He carried a .44 Colt with a cropped barrel in a leather hip pocket built for it. His pasty face livened slightly, less unhappy, a shade hopeful, welcoming a long overdue showdown and the chance at last to beat a dismally losing game.

Soft Duval came in, but made no noticeable preparations. He always kept a couple of two-shot derringers stowed somewhere handy in his coat for short-sports and flare-ups, so he wasn't going to take off his coat and leave himself naked. He didn't show any surprise at seeing George with his hat on, although that was unique at this time of day.

At the front doors Od glanced around at Soft and George. They came on his heels. He started to shake his head and speak to them, but their eyes met his and he chopped it off.

They pushed out the swing doors and walked down the street, leaving the Avalon untended. Over at the livery stable young Ted Sieker called urgently, "Hey, wait a minute — !"

Od shook his head at Ted. A good boy, Ted. Good friend, after all, loyal, and fool enough to want to chip in because he had seen what the Jims had done to the smiling, harmless, shabbily genteel Duke. Ted, like most broadminded folk, liked that hard-drinking Britisher who never let out his name although his family had cut him adrift. But Ted didn't have the gun *sabe* for a shoot-out in fast company. He was only around eighteen and had run away from a farm somewhere back East. Just a boy.

Pacing up the street, Od found himself thinking of his own boyhood. But life was different in those days. Texas and the world were different then, cows worthless, Texas full of them and no way to sell the critters to the world, on account of the war. All they were good for then, Od recalled, was about a cup of milk per indignant cow after she lay tied down to soak for a day or two and coyotes had jumped her hungrily bawling calf during the night and gnawed it to bones.

And young Od running out to passing bands of Tonks — Tonkawa Indians, surly and hostile — to beg a nursing mother to give the baby sister a suck at her full breasts. The boy-man was that desperate. Curiously, a Tonk woman generally came through, although the bucks glowered.

Baby sister died, and Ma died, and Pa never came home from the war. The boy-man, Od Thornton, struck out east toward New Orleans, a faraway town he had heard of ever since he could understand talk. He got side-tracked to Natchez, and in the stinking alleys he got his town education.

It was several years before he returned to Texas, which by then had carved trails north to sell cows to the world and grown prosperous. He returned with some money and gambling sense and soon won a respected gunfighting reputation. He feared nothing but his old enemy, poverty. He had picked up George in San Angelo during a brief stay there; they happened to leave simultaneously at the end of a three-card game in a crowded *cantina*, both winners and the lamps shot out in the ruckus, and they drifted on together casually toward Trailtown and greener pastures.

But now, walking down Trailtown's main street, those greener pastures looked brown and lifeless. Except for Tolliver's freight wagons and a few horses tied to hitchracks, the street showed empty. Some talk rumbled behind half-closed doors. The town had long foreseen a showdown. The betting favored the Jims. They kept a hard bunch of bouncers on the payroll, headed by Tom Brien, an ex-Ranger turned gunhand.

There were other reasons for the town putting Od on the short end of the betting. Some people said he'd been living the soft life too long, that now he'd never be able to stand up in a showdown. Well, Od thought, George had hinted the same thing, and maybe they'd been right about him. He guessed, though, that some minds would be changed now. The old Od Thornton was about to take over.

George and Soft lagged behind a bit, and Od struck on ahead until he could see past the freight wagons to the front of the Silver Palace. He saw Jim Bloud and Jim Kerry. They stood together at the front door, Tom Brien hovering behind them, wearing double-gun harness. Tom Brien evidently hadn't found time to rouse up the bunch this early in the day.

Although they stood out stark against the glaring white front, the three men gazed at Od without any special sign of tightening nerves. Jim Bloud showed only a trace of his former wary belligerence. His partner, Jim Kerry, wore his usual look of bored indifference. Even Tom Brien missed by a fraction the air of a sharply ready gunman. It was as though the end of this affair was a foregone conclusion.

Od halted and said to them, "You know what I'm here for!"

He held his right hand placed exactly right. George veered over and took a wagon for cover, his short-barrel

.44 poking out. Soft trotted to the boardwalk on that side and brought up an ugly little snub-nose.

Then Heze Johns sang out, "Hold it!" He stalked from his office.

Heze Johns was not alone. He had with him his two deputies and the night marshal. The four of them held double-barreled shotguns.

Heze Johns said, "You'd sure be foolish to argue with eight loads of buckshot!" He said it to all of them, but his eyes rested on Od.

Od swung his head and looked at him. George pocketed his .44 and Soft made his derringer disappear. The Jims and Tom Brien gazed at the shotguns, not unhappily. Jim Kerry even sent the marshal a faint smile, and he was a man who rarely allowed his sharply angular face to express approval or much of anything else.

In a minute Od said, "Heze, I guess we know now whose dog you are! The collar shows plain." He watched Heze Johns's face stiffen and flush, and then he walked back to the Avalon.

George and Soft were drinking quietly with Od in the barroom when Heze Johns hit the doors gently and came in.

Seeing who it was, in the back-bar mirror, Od told George, "Give our town marshal a drink on the house. Professional courtesy. He's professionally connected with the Silver Palace!"

Heze Johns cocked a mean eye at the drink that George poured for him. He waited until George and

Soft moved off down the bar, and asked Od, "D'you believe that?"

Od looked at him. "Why not? We could've taken the Jims. They hadn't had time to set a deadfall. It promised a pretty square fight, till you bulged in with your deputies and the night man. You were right on tap. Don't tell me it was by chance, damn you!"

Heze Johns picked up his drink and swallowed it. He belched, and said reflectively, "Look. You know this ain't just a piddlin' squabble for trade between a coupla saloons. It's more'n that to me, anyhow. A lot more. I'm marshal here."

"I put you in," Od reminded him. "Three years ago. No, four."

"Five," Heze corrected. "You were king of this town then and I was your man. You ran this place square. You gave the boys a fair shake for their money. You sent 'em off up the trail on time, sober — well, sober enough. I've seen you shut down tight for three days, to make 'em push on, when the trail bosses asked you."

He sighed, staring down at his emptied glass. "You had respect. So did I. This town had a good name."

"Not any more. It's got a worse name now than even Fort Griffin ever had, and that's saying plenty."

"I know. The old name's forgot. They call this Trailtown, now. The shippers threaten they'll shun-trail way round, if we don't clean up. So do the freighters and the stage-line. If they do it, this town will shrivel up and blow away like tumbleweed in a prairie wind."

"Who's to blame?" Od demanded. "Who favored letting the Jims in? A little competition, you said,

14

wouldn't hurt the Avalon. So the Jims opened the Silver Palace — a honkytonk with everything thrown in. It's a hell-hole that's got too hot for you to plug up. They've taken the town over. This morning I might have put a stop to it. That chance won't come again." He lighted a cigar, and asked deliberately, "What do the Jims pay you?"

For a minute Heze Johns stood silent. Then he expelled a long breath and rubbed his nose as if it were cold. "You make it hard to talk to you," he said. "Sure — the Jims knew you'd be out for 'em, after what was done to the Duke. I knew too. They asked me to be on hand. I was. I'll tell you why."

"When Gloria quit to the Silver Palace, her excuse was —"

"Shut up!" Heze snapped. "Listen! Complaints against this town have reached the governor, from the big shippers whose herds get stalled here. Not to mention the robberies and riots and killings, let alone the boys who're sick — and they're *sick* when the Silver Palace turns 'em loose! You know what I mean. They never learn. Broke and *sick!*"

"I know. Next trip they're back for more. The big whirl. Rotgut whisky, knock-outs, and those near-naked women —"

"Yeah," Heze said. "Your Avalon never gave 'em anything the like of it. But over at Tascosa, Judge Parker don't know that. He's got a squad of deputy U.S. marshals working out of his office this year. He's got orders to send 'em in with open warrants, very next time there's a killing here."

"Open warrants?"

"Right! And you know how it is. The last man gets it. Like the little boy caught robbing the apple orchard, he gets the whipping for the whole gang. I did once."

"So did I," Od recalled aloud. "I was a skinny kid, and the man's damned switch took the hide off my —" He broke it off, thinking. "Judge Parker, eh?"

Heze nodded. "Parker. Ray Bowers is head marshal — and he's no friend o' yours. Did I cross you this morning, or did I do you a favor?"

Od looked at him. He hadn't really believed that Heze had sold out to the Jims. That had been bitter anger speaking. Heze did pull some boners, but he was square. He couldn't fool a blind mule.

"I'm sorry," Od said to him. "I owe you a favor."

"You do," Heze agreed. "Want to pay it back?"

"Anything in reason, yes."

"That your word?"

"I've said it. What the hell d'you want?"

Heze bobbed his head. "Thank you. I want this town back. Till I came here five years ago, I never got to be more'n a deputy, any place. Something always went wrong. Here, everything went right. I was doing a good job as marshal, and I was respected. I could see the town growing. Given a chance, it'd get big and important some day." He coughed self-consciously. "Maybe I'd be mayor then."

Od acknowledged the remote possibility with a slight rise of his eyebrows. Vanity could crop up in the most unlikely soil.

16

The marshal went on: "I want rid of the Jims as much as you do. But I don't want you to hang for doing it, because I'll need your help later to put the town to rights."

Od grinned at the blunt self-interest. A small taste of prestige had whetted Heze's appetite; but it would never be satisfied — he wasn't bright enough. Heze was one of those people who saw no possible connection between bad luck and poor judgment. He repeated his mistakes, like the trail drivers who returned to the Silver Palace, got skinned again, and each time departed cursing the town.

Heze took Od's grin to signify approval. He grinned back. "The Jims won't last long now," he predicted. "Not a week passes without fights in the Silver Palace. Somebody gets shot and ten witnesses swear it was in self-defense. Judge Parker's only waiting to pounce on the next one. If there ain't somebody killed soon, Parker will settle for an assault and robbery — and them we get most any night! I got the word."

It sounded cynical enough to ring right — wait for another murder and use the corpse to trigger in the big law — but Od said, "If the Jims find out Parker's ready to send in Ray Bowers's squad —"

Heze shook his head positively. "I got the word strictly private and official. From the marshals' camp at Tascosa. As town marshal here, I was 'titled to know. I'm working with 'em. It'll go off smooth, soon's there's another rumpus. Only trouble is you."

"Me, eh? Like this morning?"

"Well, yeah. Besides, Ray Bowers has been waiting to pin something on you for years. He's a mighty ambitious man, and you were always the big fish he needed to make him even more important than Judge Parker. You made a fool of Bowers for a long time, but now you're scraping bottom and plenty of people in this town aren't too unhappy about it. They're going to hell, maybe, but they like it, and they remember how you put the lid on things here. First real trouble, Bowers will pin it on you, and there'll be plenty to back him up. You'll just have to go off for a couple weeks till things are settled and we can take hold."

"Run out, eh?" Od said angrily. "Damn you, Heze —"

"Damn *you!*" snapped Heze, raising his voice and suddenly out of temper. "You owe me a favor and you gave me your word! The night stage north comes through around nine. I ask you to take it, for the good o' the town and all of us!"

Od didn't like it, but he had to admit Heze made sense. Besides, he hadn't turned up anything at Fort Griffin to help his business. Maybe somewhere else he'd find just the right attraction — some woman — to do the job. And when he came back, if Bowers still was looking for trouble, well, damn him, he'd find it.

The night stage dusted in on time, though not with the grand flourish of the day stage — the driver knew the audience would be smaller at this hour. Six horses stamped to a standstill outside the livery. Ted Sieker, a darting ghost in the yellow light of the coach lamps,

18

changed teams, and the driver grumped, "All set, ready to roll!" He had an empty coach under him, no fares for him to lord it over.

Od threw a light valise up and climbed up after it, taking his seat beside the driver. To the driver he said, "Nobody else. Let's go." The driver looked at him. Od said, "Get rolling, or hand me the lines and I'll drive."

The driver whirled his long lash and the stagecoach lurched as the fresh horses hit the collars. The battered Concord bounced past Havens' Hardware and Bateman's Grocery, and swerved to the middle of the street to avoid the freight wagons outside Tolliver's depot.

Od remembered when the street was uncrowded, just a cattle trail with the Avalon sticking up alone beside it and empty country all around. Things grew up fast in this country. They died fast, too, sometimes. He liked this big Panhandle strip that Texas jutted so cockily north. Its temper and quick tempo suited him.

He heard the blare of the Silver Palace, running full blast on a song-and-dance blue turn accompanied by the clatter of roulette balls, poker chips, dice, glasses, and roars of drunken cheering. The girls on-stage were probably running the usual stripping contest to get the night started at full steam. Well, that was all right for fun, but as a business . . . No. Not for a man. For a madam.

The Silver Palace stood ninety feet broad and its front windows spread out a fan of light that made black streaks of the street's ruts. Past the tall freight wagons the Concord rolled full into the light.

The light threw both front corners of the place into deep shadow, but Od caught a move at the north corner and he said to the driver, "Duck over!"

"Uh?" Although by now the driver plainly sensed risk, he balked at obeying a mere fare, especially one who had already annoyed him. Then a gun-flash speared out of the dark corner and the startled horses shied from the loud report, and he ducked over almost onto his knees.

Od fired past the driver, and twisted around and slammed his second shot close over the top of the stagecoach. He glimpsed a dark figure rock sidewise and a pale glint of metal that slewed around and upward, erratically, as the man took his spill. The stagecoach bounced on. Cursing, the driver came upright, fingering the lines, getting the running team back in hand.

A mile out of town the driver got the team halted. His cursing reached artistry when he found he'd lost his whip, and till he ran out of breath. "Somebody's after us," he told Od sourly. "On a horse. Friend o' yours?"

"I hear him. We'll find out." Od sent back a hail. "Who's coming, there?"

"Me!" sang out Heze Johns. He overshot the halted stagecoach in the dark, and swung around and rode back to it. "Od, you played hell! Did you have to do that?"

"Some Silver Palace joker took a crack at me," Od said. "I think I got him. Hope it was Jim Bloud."

"It was Tom Brien," Heze said. "You only nicked his shinbone, but it's like to started a riot, ev'body waving guns around crazy. If you're all right, you better travel on — and stay away a month!"

He heeled his horse. "By that time," he called back hopefully, "somebody's bound to 'a' got killed! Bowers'll clean up the town and we'll be on top again!"

"Hold the town till I get back," Od called after him. To the driver he said, "Let's get rolling, eh?"

"That damn town's too ornery to live," growled the driver, booting off the brake and line-slapping the team. "I hear it was okay once, but I don't believe it."

"I knew it when it was. It'll be okay again."

"Huh!" grunted the driver skeptically. "Where you bound?"

"Central City."

"Colorado. The mining country, eh? That," vowed the driver, "is where I'd go if I had a stake. To hell with this goddam Texas and partic'ly this Panhandle!"

"I like this Panhandle. My stake's in it. I'll be coming back here soon."

"Yeah? Well — it ain't illegal to be crazy, I always say!"

Od nodded gravely. "It's a tough country." He punched the empty shells from his gun and thumbed in fresh cartridges from his belt-loops. "It ain't illegal to be crazy about Texas, is what I always say."

"You musta been born here."

"Right by Galveston Bay. Close to San Jacinto."

"That," stated the driver, "explains it! Once a Texan, always a —"

"That's right," Od said.

CHAPTER
TWO

Eureka Street, churned to mud by the constant traffic, promised a disaster to any pedestrian stepping off the slippery boardwalks. Only one crossing remained, where the street humped over a stony patch, and that required some careful footwork if you wanted to reach the other side without a bootful of mud.

Od joined the line there, stuffing his trouser legs inside his high Texas boots in readiness. As he did so, bending over, the front brim of his hat touched the back of the girl ahead of him in the line.

The girl straightened perceptibly at the touch, but she didn't turn her head. Od couldn't see her face; and having been up all night he wasn't much interested. He wanted to get back to his room in the Teller House, to a bath and some sleep. The Teller House, newest hotel in Central City, had hot water and inside flush-commodes and adjustable windows to every room.

"Pardon," he murmured to the girl. His eyes checked her in absently: blue dress and a hat. She gave no response, and still didn't turn.

Lady, he thought. Ought to be men-folks with her, husband or brother or somebody. This town. And the mud. Not right, lady out alone.

It was her turn to cross Eureka Street. She hesitated, fingering her blue skirt, lifting it an inch or two, taking a step off the boardwalk, then retreating when the mud threatened to cover her shoe — a foolishly low shoe, not much more than a slipper, and quite shabby. She glanced quickly over her shoulder. Something evidently persuaded her to risk it. She lifted her skirt a little higher and for an instant stood poised like a diver, or like a bird about to take flight, leaning forward and her arms bent outward. Od, finishing tucking in his trousers, got a close view of neat bare ankles, and a little more, below petticoat ruffles.

Somebody raised a disturbance, shoving past the waiting line and bumping Od aside. Coming erect, Od recognized him as one of the men he had gambled with during the night.

The others had called him Chico, a weird name for a man who obviously wasn't Mexican and certainly not little; tall and thick-bodied, he wore his fair hair long, old frontier fashion. He was reaching for the girl, his big hands scooping low, for the girl wasn't very tall. Od's elbow caught him in the neck, a driving jab in the muscles beneath the ear. Some man in the jostled line snorted a surprised laugh.

Od slid his hands under the armpits of the blue dress and picked the girl up off her feet and waded on through the mud and over the street, carrying her before him. She was light. His hands told him that she didn't wear a corset. No stockings, no corset, shabby shoes. And those petticoats were cheap cotton, not linen.

24

No perfume, either, that he could detect. She smelled female. As unmistakable as the odor of a house that had a new baby in it. Clean, but there it was and all the soap in creation couldn't get rid of it.

He heard the man who had laughed say, "Can't blame a man for tryin'! Seen her at the opry?"

After a gasp and a stiffening, the girl didn't fight, didn't wriggle. She hung rigid, clamping her arms tight down on Od's supporting hands as if to imprison them from exploring her breasts. Which was just as well, because the footing was bad and Od had to dodge through a string of ore wagons from the Gunnell Hills.

But when he set her down safely on her feet on the far side, she said, "You — !" The word she used was pungent, but she delivered it in a low tone, loaded with utter fury.

Then she whirled around, and all at once her face and eyes said she'd made a mistake — he wasn't the one she thought he was.

And Od stood tongue-tied for once, staring down at her. She had a pile of reddish-brown hair, and white skin, faint shadows under violet-blue eyes that seemed translucent and were just slightly slanted inward, and full lips and a rounded chin. Dainty shape of body, a bit wide at the hips. But those details he didn't check in until later, from her picture in his memory.

All he was aware of now were her eyes, her female smell, and the tingling in his hands that suddenly rippled all through him. He snatched off his broad-brimmed hat and bowed to her, conscious of nothing except her. This mining town, the all-night gambling, the mud and the big blond man — that all belonged to a year ago, to a thousand years ago.

This was an entirely new feeling. Amazed, he heard his own voice say calmly, "Glad to be of slight service to you, Miss — uh — ?" As if she were one more woman, and he on the make for her as usual.

She regarded him, at last saying in a curiously guarded and small voice, "Thank you." She glanced across Eureka Street and said again, "Thank you." Then she was gone, hurrying, almost running down toward the lower end of town.

The blond man came on over. He let his gaze go all around before bringing it to rest thoughtfully on Od. In the end he did nothing; just walked off without a word. But his look promised there would be more than words — and soon.

The canvas sign hung bedraggled in the rain, bravely announcing that tonight the Royal European Grand Opera Repertory Company had the honor to present *Roméo et Juliette — de Gounod*.

Last and Final Appearance! was scrawled in crayon at the bottom. *Grand Benefit Performance! All Seats $1*. For whose grand benefit it didn't say, but nothing in booming Central City cost less than a dollar, so the price wasn't worth any quibble.

Od paid his dollar to a stoutish lady at the door, who swept dark eyes over him and complimented his presence with more than a nod. She had impossibly blue-black hair and eyebrows. Od returned a bow, and was rewarded with a flash of large white teeth and an expert flutter of long eyelashes. Her hand gestured him in gracefully. Shedding his oiled slicker, shaking rain off his hat, stamping mud from his boots, Od went on inside.

He measured at a glance the sorry worth of this place that somebody had named importantly the Victoria Hall. For a moment he stood frowning, his dripping hat and slicker in his hands, wondering if he had got hooked into a blue show for yahoos, men only.

But that girl — she wouldn't be in —

A lonely piano tinkled somewhere in the semi-darkness. Bright paint brushed sparely here and there only accentuated the makeshift character of the Victoria Hall. Plain wooden benches served as seats. There was no bar; its lack explained the scanty patronage, Od supposed. A music-hall without beer went against all tradition. As impractical as a ship without an ocean. But this was an opera, he remembered. Different thing.

Only about a dozen men made up the audience, all miners, hairy and dirty in their working clothes, some stretched out asleep on the benches, others puffing short pipes and mumbling together. They had done their drinking before wandering in here out of the rain, that was clear. Od took a seat and lit up a cigar. The good tobacco helped kill other odors. A sign pleaded vainly, *No Smoking Please*.

The curtain rolled up, after a false start, to expose a tiny stage fixed out to represent the interior of an Italian palace. Weak lighting and tattered scenery dimmed the effect, but with a little imagination one could catch onto the idea.

A bunch of people surged on-stage into the thick cloud of pipe smoke pouring over the footlights, dressed to the nines in satins and feathers, all singing in a foreign language while the piano player tried to sound like a full orchestra.

The slumbering miners stirred awake, grunting and making noises. One, the only one not wearing a hat, stood, swore loudly, and sat down again, scratching his scalp and staring. The act bellowed on.

Od shifted uneasily on the hard bench, embarrassed, wishing he hadn't come. Those people up there were probably doing their honest best, but it was no good. He recognized among them the dark lady who had taken his dollar at the door. She was up front, a duchess or such, clarioning forth and fanning smoke away by making extravagant hand gestures. She sure was trying her damnedest.

Od had attended the opera one time in New Orleans. There it had a place. Good bet. But grand opera for drunken, work-weary miners — he wouldn't have backed it at any odds. These people, though, had chanced it.

He saw a shining confidence on the face of the dark lady as she held a high note. Hell, they still believed they were good. Maybe they were, for all he knew, but what he liked was the plain nerve of them. Grand Benefit Performance. Last show, for a dozen fuddled apes in a patched-up barn, and giving their best to it although the take wouldn't buy them a dinner and some of them looked as if they could do with a good meal. He admired their guts.

28

Then he sat motionless, completely intent and absorbed, again tingling all through his body as he had that morning. He did not blink his eyes, for fear of missing a fraction of a motion, and the cigar in his fingers dribbled less and less smoke and finally went out.

The shivaree had melted off, and she — that girl — sang alone on the stage, danced alone while singing, and the stage seemed to blaze alight and the lonely piano *was* an orchestra.

She wore a little cap, rhinestone spangled. And a blue satin gown with a high and close-fitting bodice and full skirt. The miners were suddenly very quiet.

When she finished, Od slowly relaxed, rubbing his eyes and breathing deeply. His legs and his back felt stiff, as if he had overtaxed the muscles with a vast effort sustained too long. He wiped his face with a handkerchief, and muffled a cough. His throat was dry.

He tried to follow what was going on, but that was like trying to recapture a blazing sunrise after it had bleached out. The miners reverted to their noisy restlessness, yawning and talking aloud. Their rising tones carried a hint of dull resentment; they disliked what they couldn't understand. The hatless one sat sorting out loose change from his pockets.

The scene now showed all the company again, with the addition of a fellow wearing velvet and a feather in his cap. That fellow seemed unpopular with the bunch, for no clear reason. However, the girl leaned all the other way and made up to him — and that was a hard one to figure, for he was too fat to give her much of a chase and maybe too old to get up enough steam for it.

Being veteran players, they must have sensed the growing hostility of their audience. Still, they struggled on, only two or three of them betraying slight signs of nervousness. Od wished that they'd all track out and let the girl take over. That could save it.

The fat fellow in velvet sang a piece, the girl sang back at him, and it seesawed to and fro until the others took a hand and chipped in their singing opinion of the matter. The dark lady gestured and they all crowded to the footlights, facing the audience, singing loúd enough to be heard at Casto.

This was their big chip. This, their expressions said, must win over any audience.

Their faces actually shone, able in an instant to triumph over tired discouragement and despair and fear. Grand Benefit Performance. *This time — perhaps they'll like us! Perhaps we can stay on, make a go of it!* Last and Final Appearance. Last chance.

The hatless miner reared up. His muscular right arm made a violent back-and-forth swing. He hurled a handful of coins into their faces and shouted, "Goddam stinkin' Eyetalians, shut up!"

The miners whooped, and began scrambling around for other missiles to throw. Benches crashed over.

The singing wavered hideously, voices dragging, breaking, and trailed off. The man in velvet obstinately kept on a bit longer to end a long note, clutching his eye that had been struck hard by a coin, and bowed briefly and retreated.

The rest backed off-stage with him. Their faces now showed hopeless defeat. The curtain fell hastily, got stuck and hung askew. Many hands rippled it and punched it from the stage side, forcing it down. A thrown bench-leg drummed against it, breaking a rip in it. The piano quit.

The hatless miner stood laughing. Od walked down to him, pulled him around, and hit him between the belt and his chest. The miner caved in, gasping and jerking. Nobody noticed, in the uproar.

Od walked on, climbed onto the stage, and brushed past the edge of the curtain. The stage lay empty, backdrop and wings more tattered at close view than appeared from out front. He turned right, and came upon them.

They huddled together, the front rank composed of the fat tenor and the girl and the dark lady. Od guessed they were set to fight him and the miners and all Central City. Like cats, cornered and desperate, against a dog pack.

He swept off his hat to them. He said with gentle courtesy and a dash of necessary cheek, "I am Colonel Odum P. Thornton, at your service." He was no more a colonel than dead Lincoln's hat.

They held off, seeing him as a tall and dangerous-looking man, darkly somber in his dignity.

"I am a lover of music," he added. He had discovered it since listening to the girl sing.

The dark lady came forward a pace, saying, "I am Madame Ferrari, Colonel."

Her large eyes took him in, as they had done at the door, approving him. And yet, Od guessed, Madame Ferrari wasn't fooled by him much. Taking his hand, she said frankly, "You find us in ruin, as you see. Our manager skipped out. Two weeks ago — no, Mario?"

The fat tenor replied, "Two weeks and a day. With the money, and little of that, *tiens!*" He bowed to her and to Od. "She since is manager."

Od murmured that she did well — tariff-taker at the door and singing on-stage to boot. Pretty full occupation. He looked at the girl.

"Goddam!" said Mario. "These people! These wild Indians!"

He had a bruise under his left eye where the coin had struck him. They, the company, would accept throw-money, he assured Od. They were too poor to show insult, *comprenez?* "But — pennies!" — showing them in his hand. He hadn't neglected to gather them up. "Pennies!"

"With such a force," Madame Ferrari put in. She sighed. "This night we thought to be good. Rain. So many people, this town, no place to go."

"Twenty or more saloons and gambling houses," Od said. "And the wrestling matches and rock-drilling contests. Tough competition." Best not to mention the other amusements. With the mines running double-shift at Gunnell Hills and Casto and Quartz, Central City strained itself to please the tastes of all comers.

Madame Ferrari's expressive eyes conveyed to Od a perfectly good understanding of Od's omission. "Yes, of course. It is our misfortune that we try to lift up —"

"So we are bust!" broke in Mario. "We owe for this shed the rent, which belong to the Mrs. Wright, and her brother he is telling us alla time —"

Mrs. Wright ran the big red-light house around the corner from the Victoria Hall. Od had learned that the gambler they called Chico — Chico Avery — was loosely supposed to be her brother.

Madame Ferrari shushed Mario with a regal sweep of her arm. "The Colonel does not possess interest in the troubles of us," she told him.

But she eyed Od hopefully. They all did. He had a well-to-do air, and in their wretched poverty they worshipped the most casual nod from prosperity. Yesterday he had sold his diamond, and last night's gambling had swelled the stake.

He looked straight at the girl. She gazed past him at the empty stage. The miners evidently were settling down to get back to sleep, which was mainly what they had come in for.

He said, stretching a point, "I'm in show business, myself."

"Ah!" breathed Madame.

The girl shortened her gaze to Od's face, scanning it coolly as though searching for truth. She was by far the youngest member of this stranded troupe, yet Od received at that moment a distinct impression that in some ways she was the wisest. She was not allowing her credulity to be blinded by hope.

In sheer defense Od said, "I own the celebrated Avalon, down in —" He almost said Trailtown, and

33

caught himself. "In Texas. In the town that bears my name Thornton."

It had borne his name for a while, anyhow, and he reckoned it would again. By now Judge Parker must have sent in the marshals to clean out the Jims and their crowd. He would rule the roost again and soon build up the Avalon better than ever.

Detecting his interest, Madame led Od over to the girl. "You must meet our Juliette. Mademoiselle Beri Rheipneure. We thought she was quite wonderful tonight. We had taken liberties with the score, to make simple. No prologue. Liberties most grave — but in this horrible place who knows opera? Who knows French?"

"Who, indeed?" Od said. He didn't, for one.

To Mlle. Beri Rheipneure he said awkwardly, trying to pick up Madame's foreign twist of words, "Quite wonderful I thought, too, you, tonight." He bowed, hat in hand. Madame and the rest discreetly moved off a short distance.

"Mamzell," said Od, "I — uh — possess the interest in the song and the dance of you." He was catching onto the trick of it. "To make short, I felt you — felt it — with such a force —"

He stopped. She was actually laughing at him, with her chin tucked in and head bent, sort of chuckling down into her bosom, and he thought he heard her say, "You'll trip in a minute!" The laughter turned her into an imp.

"Beg your pardon," he muttered.

She raised her face. "No, I beg your pardon." After swallowing a last chuckle, she said, "You looked so funny I couldn't help it. My name's really Berry Ripner. I was born in Minnesota."

He blew a sigh of relief, and took both her hands. "That's better! I wasn't doing so good, eh?"

"No. But you tried hard. It was a strain." She glanced down at his hands holding hers.

He saw her coolness returning, and that he couldn't allow. "A strain on us both. How about these others — are they fakes, too?"

She shook her head. "No. Genuine foreigners." Her eyes met his squarely. "All genuine. They're my friends."

Her look and tone of voice expressed an almost scornful doubt of his understanding.

He released her hands, saying, "They strike me as good folks. Just a bit different, is all."

"A bit different," she agreed coldly. "They're not savages, so they're different. So they're 'goddam stinking Eyetalians', despised and stranded way out here in this sinkhole! How far is it back to New York? Two thousand miles? Three thousand? Perhaps they'll try to walk it."

"How about you?"

She put on a bright stage smile, false as a painted mask. "Oh, I'm more lucky. I'm young. I have a very pressing offer to work in Mrs. Wright's —"

"Cut that out!" he told her harshly. Sounds of movement disturbed the quietness of the hall, and he heard members of the opera troupe whispering. "The part doesn't suit you." He reached to take her hands, but she whisked them behind her and drew back.

She was standing like that, on the defensive, white-faced and blazing-eyed, when two men flung open the curtain and clumped onto the stage. Madame Ferrari moaned, "Ah!" and Mario dramatically slapped his hand to the silly tin dagger dangling from his stout waist. The rest of the troupe froze.

The two were Chico Avery and the hatless miner who had broken up the show.

No actor could have made a more ponderously deliberate entrance than Chico Avery. His large size and very wide eyes, as much as his manner, helped create the illusion of a calm giant. He paused to glance about, slowly. Tonight he flaunted fringed buckskins and a hugely sweeping hat, a pair of pearl-handled guns in fine new holsters, and a ten-inch knife stuck in an Indian sheath. He was Sam Houston and Kit Carson, larger than life, with touches of Wild Bill a-gettin' his picture took.

Followed by the miner, Chico Avery waded through the troupe; weeds beneath his feet, these foreigners.

Due to the poor lighting and the shadows, he failed to notice Od until alongside of him. He pulled up abruptly. His full, handsome face grew lean at the cheeks. He looked around at the miner, who nodded.

The miner inspected Od carefully as he slid his right hand into his coat pocket. Od wondered what other methods Chico Avery had employed to ruin the show, on other nights. Those pennies had not been flung on drunken impulse.

Chico Avery marched onward two paces, which took him so close to the girl that the massive buckle of his two-gun buscadero belt touched her. She didn't retreat, but her mouth and jaw thinned and in that moment she wasn't beautiful at all; even her eyes blanked over like marbles.

From his great height Chico Avery roared down at her, "See how it is? Show's busted! Where's the rent? Ten times I've told you no deadbeats put it over on Chico! I gave you plenty chance to make good! I guess now you'll come with me and talk it over!"

Od shifted his feet. The miner whipped a brass-knuckled fist up at his face. Madame Ferrari yelled a warning.

Od back-stepped, dodged the brass knuckles, and his hand hooked the bruiser by the back of his thick neck and wrenched him around. He gave him a knee hard in the groin.

The bruiser gasped, his right hand flailing high. Od drove his left fist dead-center below the chest, in the exact spot where he had hit him before, and dropped him.

Chico Avery was swinging around when Od's gun-muzzle rammed him in the spine. He uttered a pained, "Ugh!" and threw his hands shoulder high.

Prodding him ungently, Od said to the girl, "Pull his pretty guns, please. We don't want any *real* trouble here!"

He was pleased at the nimble way she did it, and at her change of face. She must have thought Chico Avery the biggest man in the Rockies. Most likely the whole troupe had thought so.

He said to Chico Avery, "Now, you Buntline hero — you Arbuckle coupon — gather up your trash and haul it out! This, I mean!" He kicked the groaning bruiser. On after-thought, he also kicked Chico Avery on the bulge of his buckskin pants. "Jump to it, boy!"

Chico Avery picked up his bruiser, with hardly a grunt of exertion, and slung him over his shoulder. He wasn't entirely a counterfeit, for he looked at Od and said, "This ain't the last of it!"

"Don't push your luck," Od advised him. "You're getting off easy. I could resent your attitude toward the lady."

"She's got a debt to settle, and I swear she'll work —"

"No," Od drawled. "She's under contract." He shoved Chico Avery on his way. "Get out!"

The big man sucked a shuddering breath. "This ain't the last of it!" he said again, and lumbered off with his burden.

After he had gone, after the silence, the girl said to Od, "So I am under contract. To you? Excuse me, I forget the terms."

"Five hundred a month."

Gloria had cost him more than that, one way and another, not counting the gold tiara.

The listening members of the troupe whooshed awed breaths. Od looked at them, made a rough estimate, and added, "And a thousand in advance, for binder."

The girl, too, looked at the troupe.

"Yes, Colonel," she said steadily. "I am under contract to you." She hesitated, then asked, "A thousand dollars in advance? When —"

"Right now," Od said, "of course."

It dug a serious hole in his stake. But he knew why she wanted it, and what she would do with it. Three thousand miles was a long walk.

They had been camping back-stage in the Victoria Hall, like tramps, living on what cheap scraps of food they could buy. The manager had deserted and left them only the stage wardrobe, which included about all the clothes they had left.

Od moved them all into the Teller House. It required persuasion and bribery. The Teller House, towering four floors high, was newly built for moneyed people who demanded and could afford the best.

The members of the stranded and poverty-stricken opera troupe cut rather odd figures in the lobby, in their shabby satins and velvets. But they sailed in grandly and let the speechless bellboys usher them to their rooms.

That night the hotel manager called on Od in his room. He beat around the bush a while before he came out with what was troubling him. "We can't have the Teller House turned into a shooting gallery," he informed Od. "Mr. Avery and his friends are on the watch for you."

"Get the sheriff," Od advised him.

"Mr. Avery is a deputy sheriff," the hotel manager mentioned.

"That," said Od, "does make a difference."

Later on, Od trod the carpeted hallway to the girl's room. He tapped on the door, heard her say, "Come in," and entered.

The bedcovers were mussed. She had been luxuriating in a real bed, the first in a long time. She sat upright on the edge of the bed now, wearing a thin gown, expecting a maid with fresh towels or some such rare luxury.

Her warm young loveliness, with sleepiness flushing her face and seeming to soften her eyes to a quiet passion of desire, beckoning and promising, wiped out all of Od's experienced understanding of women. Had she been any other girl, no matter how lovely and enticing, he would have known the precise method of approach, the gentle pursuit, leading to an inevitable surrender. But such guile required a certain detachment, which was impossible for him now.

He walked straight to her and took her in his arms without any preliminaries. He had never done this in all his life; but he had never till now fallen headlong in love with any of his women.

In five seconds he retreated from a fighting wildcat, his face hammered and clawed by small fists and fingernails.

"You uncivilized brute!" she spat at him, huddled in a ball of fury on the bed. "You — you Texas savage!" She shook back her tousled hair with a fling of her head, and in that moment it was she who looked the savage.

He managed to stammer, "I beg your pardon!" and wiped a hand over his scratched face. He looked at his hand and saw a smear of blood on it. Anger — at himself as well as at her — choked his exclamation down to a spare, "Goddam!"

She said tightly, every word sharp and staccato, "You have not bought me! If I had chosen to sell myself, there was Chico Avery and Mrs. Wright's house!"

He forced down his anger. "You shouldn't wear a flimsy nightgown like that when you let a man in your room! For that matter, you shouldn't ever let — well, never mind that now. I came to tell you we take the early train to Denver in the morning. And south out of there to Trinidad, quick, and the first stage we can get down to Texas."

"Why?" she asked, tugging the bedclothes up over herself.

He shrugged. "Chico Avery is law," Od said, "and he's after me, he and his pals." He gave a further thought to it. "He's after you, too, though in another way." He turned to the door. "I'll give you a call around five in the morning. I'll knock on the door."

The door opened before he reached it. Madame Ferrari came in. Her dark eyes flitted from Od to the girl, and back again.

Od said to her with partly suppressed anger, "Good evening, Madame!" He passed by her, and at the door he said to the girl, without looking back at her, "Five in the morning."

"I shall be ready," she told him.

With the door shut and Od gone, she said to Madame Ferrari, "Early in the morning I catch the train with him." She spoke French. "To Texas. To a theater called the Avalon, in a town called Thornton. Who in the world even heard of it? You, Madame?"

Madame Ferrari seated and composed herself on the edge of the bed. She said, "*Ma fille*, you are a virgin, I believe?"

"Well, practically."

Madame bobbed her dyed wig. "An experiment — in very youth — it counts nothing. Now I tell you. Men have hunger for virgins. I do not know why, for with experience a woman grows — but that is aside. That man, I like him. But he is — let me say plainly — dangerous to you. Not like the Avery beast, no. But dangerous! I know men. Unless, of course, you love him. In which case —"

"No."

"Well, then. You have abstracted from him the money to carry us all back to New York, where we may obtain another booking. There is enough money for you also. Come with us back to New York!"

"Skip? It's an idea."

"You signed nothing. He gave to you the money, without legal contract. Strange, such a man . . ."

Berry yawned and stretched her arms, and Madame eyed the sleek young body enviously and thought of her own glory thirty years gone.

"No, Madame."

"Why not?" Madame looked at the girl keenly.

"I gave him my word. He accepted it." Berry curled her legs up, rested her chin on her knees, and studied her toes. "Besides," she said candidly, "I think he would catch me slipping out. Or" — she shivered — "Avery would!"

42

"All men want you, naturally. You are beautiful and young. Come with us back to New York!"

"Is New York so safe for a girl?" Berry laughed wryly, cuddling her knees. "Madame, my good friend, tomorrow all of you will start back to New York. There you will be with friends again, and get another booking. I shall go to Texas."

Madame had heard of Texas. A terrible place, worse even than this savage Colorado. "Watch that man, the Colonel. He is dangerous, *ma fille*. Dangerous!" And Berry, remembering the eager hands and wandering eyes of too many men — one in particular — reluctantly had to agree. It wasn't just that Od was a man, but that in spite of herself he excited her.

"Yes, Madame," she said, "he is dangerous. Especially for me."

CHAPTER
THREE

The train smashed out an unending racket, but the palace car rolled along in comparative quiet. The palace car had been hooked on for the benefit of Trinidad-bound cattle buyers and speculators and others who didn't mind paying the extra fare. It flaunted green plush and mirrors, iced water and a lavatory. A polished brass spittoon graced the side of every seat.

Berry had never before traveled in such luxury. On their hopeful tour west the little opera troupe had ridden the overcrowded emigrant trains, sharing food with the land-seekers, sometimes putting on an impromptu act when monotony grew intolerable and the children kept crying.

She could still see old Mario, sweating, shouting at them, "A clown, me, see? I am Mario, best goddam clown inna world! I show you!"

And if he was not too sober, not crushed by his memories of failure, then Mario was magnificently *opera bouffe*, cutting outrageous capers and singing in full voice. The kids loved it, and he loved them. They were the most generously appreciative audience he'd ever had.

The train overhauled a string of canvas-top wagons slowly straggling up the broad trail that ran parallel to the railroad right-of-way. Through the palace car window Berry could see the tired, dust-grimed faces of some of the men and women.

"Movers," commented Od, seated across from Berry. "They're heading for the lower Pecos country, I guess, to take up homesteads. The tide has lately turned that way. Somebody spread word that the Pecos Valley has good soil, water, and a warm year-round climate."

A newsboy came through the palace car, hawking candy, nut pies, pamphlets, pictures, and paper-back copies of *The Old Curiosity Shop* pirated from Dickens. Half humorously, Od asked Berry if she wanted anything from the assortment.

Berry started to shake her head, but the alert newsboy paused expectantly, so she chose a pamphlet at random. Its price was ten cents and Od gave the newsboy a dollar to get rid of him, which Berry considered to be showy extravagance; more than once a dollar had made do to feed the whole troupe. She bent close to the window to catch a last glimpse of the wagon emigrants, wondering if they had enough to eat.

"In a year or two," Od said, knowing the direction of her gaze, "the poor fools will be moving again."

She sat up straight and looked directly at him. "My folks moved to Minnesota like that, in a wagon. They were not fools!"

"Probably not," he agreed. "But I know that Pecos country. It's not Minnesota. Five years out of six down there the Pecos runs dry. The soil's all right, when the wind isn't blowing it into the next county. Warm climate, yes. Summer, you leave beef outdoors to cook! Trying to farm a country like that is stupid. It's cow-country."

"Why aren't they warned? Why don't you, for example, warn them before they get there?"

He shrugged. "You can't tell them. They have to learn."

She opened the pamphlet, her hands shaking with anger. He was hard and cynical, she felt. Any generosity had to pay off for him, she was sure. Where the prospects promised him no returns in one way or another, he gave nothing. And this was a man who — she could admit it to herself — held a frighteningly potent attraction for her.

Od saw that he had created another bad impression. He wanted to correct his mistakes with her, yet the more he pushed the worse botch he made of it. He said to her in an attempt at explanation, "In Texas you don't hand out advice till you're asked for it."

What he meant was, simply, that you gave — were expected to give, in Texas — every man credit for sense enough to go his own road. He was capable of compassion, often too much and wasted, but his tough environment made him mask the compassion under a hard casualness, easily mistaken for brutal indifference by a stranger to the West.

His brief explanation apparently did him no good, so he made another try. "Way down the lower Pecos Valley there's a place called Quemado. It used to be a little 'dobe settlement of Mexicans who raised some *frijole* beans and a few goats. Now it's a boom town. Speculators are even selling town lots. The country is filling up with fool hoemen, and the country will break them. Meantime, the Mexicans have got shoved out of Quemado — they didn't hold any legal title to their miserable little bean fields."

He spread his fingers on his knees, shrugging again. "Those land-hungry emigrants aren't the only folk to feel sorry for. It was a thin living, but Quemado was home to those *paisanos* for quite a long time."

Still Berry didn't answer. "Some of us," he said, meaning himself, "advised those old Quemado *paisanos* to secure title, file homesteads, when we saw the land-rush heading that way." He smiled wryly. "For them, it meant the Land Office, and officials, and papers to scratch their mark on. Maybe they figured it was a trick. They politely didn't bother to do it — and now they're beggars, as some of the emigrants will be."

Berry didn't raise her eyes from the pamphlet Od had bought for her. She retained her expression of chill condemnation. The sarcastic force of Od's final words had hurt his case. Her father had been a land-seeking emigrant in his time, a good and honest man; therefore emigrants were all good and honest, and those who spoke against them were scoundrels, blacklegs, renegades.

Od quit. He rested back in his plush seat, somberly regarding two men, one young and one old, who played chess with a pocket set on a folding table supplied by the porter. The two chess players appeared to be father

47

and son, but Od doubted it. He was in a mood to doubt anybody and everybody, himself included.

The pamphlet, badly printed on the cheapest gray paper, contained a collection of poetical fragments. Pamphlets bought from railroad newsboys were likely to contain anything, from bawdy jokes to Scripture. Berry read a couple of lines that caught her eye.

— *Yond Cassius has a lean and hungry look;*
He thinks too much: such men are dangerous.

She raised a brief look at Od's face, and instantly her mind likened its dark leanness to that of another man, a man who had told her that she had a natural voice that needed only a little training.

She was then fresh to the big city and she believed the modest little advertisement for talented young singers and dancers.

"I will arrange for you to meet the *maestro*," the man said. "Tonight."

And that night in a quiet little restaurant where he seemed to be well-known, the man said, "A little wine?" And she woke up in a strange room, beating him off, screaming, until finally the police came. The wine, of course, had been drug-loaded, and the man was a pimp.

The police captain at the station said, "Godamighty, you kids oughta stay home! You're pie for these fancy macks. Look, I know an old feller, he books theayter acts and he's reg'lar, y'know, he knows everybody. He might find you a spot, put you on a line to one, somethin', I dunno . . ."

Berry dozed off, thinking of that ugly beginning to her stage career — a career of setbacks and small triumphs, of struggles to climb up, but never quite rising above the level of the fallen old veterans who struggled to fall no lower.

Although performing in run-down theaters and variety halls, sometimes sharing the billing with conjurers and red-nose comedians, the veteran singers could all speak of their years of study under European *maestros*. They were kind to Berry, knowing that she had no such background and little real training. They taught her all they knew, but were sure she hadn't a chance. Who in the world ever heard of an American opera singer?

They spoke fluent French as a matter of course, as well as Italian, Spanish, and some German. And Berry had a hell of a time with her Minnesota accent in that exotic effusion of tongues.

Od, restless, picked up the pamphlet which had slid from Berry's lap. The nearness of Berry, and at the same time her remoteness, continued to disturb him. It touched him to see her sleeping, a picture of wistful helplessness, this same girl who had with such effective ferocity fought off his impulsive advance. He hoped that her sleeping meant that she was at last relaxing to the fact of his presence. But his quiet movement instantly wakened her and she sat up straight again.

He studied the pamphlet, seeking an excuse to make talk. Even an argument was better than stiff silence.

Gravely he read aloud, ignoring meter and rhythm, " 'Let me have men about me that are fat, sleek-headed men, and such as sleep o' nights' — h'm!" He shook his head. "I've known some fat thieves who I wouldn't have around *me!* The joker who wrote this didn't —"

He looked up abruptly and snapped, "Well?" to the younger of the two chess players who, apparently on his way to the lavatory, had paused by Od's seat to listen.

The youth inclined his head. "I beg your pardon, sir. It is rare that one hears a Shakespearean quotation." He had a soft voice and his features were almost effeminate. "That one is from *Julius Caesar*, of course."

"Of course," said Od, giving the pamphlet another look. "Any fool knows that!" The youth's intrusion annoyed him until he noticed Berry trying to cover a smile; a skeptical smile, but welcome. To build it up, he decided to play along. "It's pure hogwash!"

The youth fluttered a pale hand. "The 'lean and hungry look' refers to Cassius's character, not to his physical appearance. Cassius could be fat, but his lean and hungry look shows through. You are correct in saying that there are fat thieves, sir. How true! How too, too true!"

While he spoke, the older man came along the car and stopped behind him. He wore plain black broadcloth and spotless white linen, and had the benign dignity of a bishop. He clapped a hand on the youth's shoulder, and bowed to Berry and Od.

"My dear nephew is, ah, hipped on the subject of fat men," he confided, smiling. "In Denver a fat rascal neatly relieved him of a handsome sum of money, on the turn of a card. Now, now, Paul, admit it! The joke is on you!"

"I fail to see the humor in it, Uncle Orville," Paul protested. "The money I can well afford. The insolent affront I cannot forgive! The way he laughed at me!"

Berry felt sorry for him, a cultured youngster, fine-drawn and easily hurt, surrounded by sharpsters and roughnecks. She suspected that he wrote romantic poetry. His uncle, trying hard to be a bluff man of the world, only succeeded in making them both look silly.

Leaning back in his seat, Od asked amusedly, "What kind of game was it?"

"An infantile game," Uncle Orville told him, with the large indulgence of one who wished it to be understood that all tricks were crystal clear to his penetrating intelligence. "A game requiring no brains, no finesse of skill or —"

"No brains, I agree," broke in Paul. "But skill, yes. Wait, let me fetch our table and I'll show you."

Uncle Orville palmed his hands upward and bent his head over sidewise. "Boys will be boys, eh? They err, and must argue that they didn't. Life is a long lesson, hard for some."

Paul returned with the folding table and set it up and placed three cards on it: the two black tens and the queen of diamonds. "The fat fellow," he explained, "mixed them up. Face-down, of course. He dared me to pick the queen, even money. I was sure I knew which one it was, but I lost."

"Three-card monte," Od said. "Right? A fool's game."

Offended, Paul picked up the three cards and shuffled them, while Uncle Orville smiled down at him. "It fooled me, sir, if that is your meaning! Can you do better?" He laid the three cards out.

Od dug into his pocket. "Twenty dollars says I can."

The train conductor entered the palace car. He halted at the table and meaningly raised his eyes to a sign that proclaimed in red print: *Passengers are hereby Warned against playing GAMES OF CHANCE with Strangers!*

Od turned up the queen and won. Uncle Orville chuckled gently at Paul. Paul plucked up the exposed queen card, frowned shortsightedly at it, and slapped it back down. In doing so he clumsily bent a corner of the card. "Shall we try it again, or does it please you to quit winner?"

"It pleases me," Od said. "But not by twenty dollars." He let his eyes fasten on the bent queen card, while Paul and Uncle Orville watched him.

Berry started a gesture as if to call attention to that tell-tale mark, and Od forestalled her, saying to Paul, "It's a dull trip. A piking game doesn't help it much. Is twenty your limit?"

"No. Make it a hundred."

"Is that money where you come from?" Od murmured, carelessly drawing out his wad of bills, fifties on the outside, at which Paul and Uncle Orville widened their eyes momentarily. "Or would it be you suffer from cold feet?"

Paul jerked bold upright. "I must resent that, sir! Uncle Orville, let me have a thousand dollars for a moment, please!" It was convincingly done, right to the last word.

"That is money," Od conceded. The conductor eyed him thoughtfully.

Paul's manipulation of the three cards this time displayed infinitely more deftness than before. He made the cards fly back and forth from hand to hand, his white fingers and manicured nails flashing in a blur of movement. Swift and sure sleight-of-hand was essential to this game. When suddenly the cards lay face-down on the table, Berry blinked her eyes before she was able to focus them on a slightly bent corner.

Od reached forward. His hand hovered for a tense and tantalizing moment over the three cards. His finger tips almost touched the bent one, then passed it by. Deliberately he turned up one of the others.

The watching train conductor expelled a sighing breath. He broke out a grin. Od's turned-up card was the queen, the elusive lady of three-card-monte fortune.

Paul's youthfulness drained out, and his face looked old and wicked. He reached under his coat. Uncle Orville said, "No!" — gesturing at the conductor and all around.

Paul stared at Od. "How did you know?"

Od scraped the money to his side of the table. "Your lean and hungry look showed through!"

"I mean the card," Paul whispered. "Did I slip up?"

"No, you did it right," Od assured him kindly. "Best I've seen in years."

"Then how — ?"

"I cut my teeth on this game when the bent-card trick was old."

"Where's your stomping ground?"

"Follow the Trinidad trail down near to Red River, and at Trailtown ask for Od Thornton of the Avalon. I'll set up the drinks or whatever's your fancy."

"It's off our run, thanks all the same. We don't like Texans, present company not excepted!"

"Matter of taste. It takes all kinds."

"Come, Paul," droned Uncle Orville sorrowfully. "We are out a thousand and twenty dollars. Let us set up our chessboard in an honest car and catch some suckers! I warned you about these palace cars, didn't I? But you are *so* ambitious."

Od slipped the twenty to the conductor, who then claimed he'd figured Od knew what he was up to with that pair of sharks and glad he was to see them taken down for once because although they made his run regularly they tipped light; not like real folks — meaning Texans — gents who passed out twenties along with a democratic handshake.

Afterward, Od remarked to Berry that his luck appeared to be running pretty well this trip and he hoped it would continue.

He regretted his words after catching the wary expression in her eyes. And he failed to relish the familiar satisfaction of having beaten a rigged game, of having met threatened violence with a defeating stare and the readiness to explode his greater violence.

He would have liked to explain to Berry the old trick of the bent card and the pale youth's expertly handled

54

switch, the technique of the come-on and the follow-through, the final pattern laid out in perfect execution to pluck the confident pigeon. But Berry leaned back and closed her eyes.

She still felt sorry for Paul, that cultured and soft-spoken youth with his beautiful hands and unworldly face. She regarded Od as an unscrupulous shark. And in Od's spoken hope for his continued good luck this trip she found a meaning that put her more than ever on guard. He was, as Madame Ferrari warned, a dangerous man. A Texas man. Steel to the core. No conscience. Under the good clothes and courteous veneer, wild as a savage.

At the station eating-house where the train stopped, Od advised Berry to order fish. Hungry passengers stampeded out of the train, but Od hurried Berry and secured seats at the cook's end of the dining-room. "Fish or eggs," he told her. "The train pulls out in half an hour."

Failing to see any relation between food and a railroad schedule, Berry ordered beefsteak. She knew she was being deliberately perverse, but she was damned if she'd let him tell her what to eat.

Her beefsteak arrived, tough as leather fried to a crisp. The blunt table knife was useless. She studied the technique of a man on her left. The man pinned his steak down with his knife and tore off pieces with the fork. She tried to emulate him, but without success; it demanded brute strength and a lot of elbow-room.

Od finished his fish. He watched her for a minute, and walked outside, lighting a cigar. Everyone had to go

55

forward on his or her own road, making the same old mistakes. Hard, but you couldn't tell them. They had to learn. Free advice, no matter how well-meant, drifted off like the dust of a desert breeze, changing nothing.

The eating-house emptied. A voice called out something, conversationally. Od strode in and lifted Berry off her seat — hands under her armpits, as he had carried her across Eureka Street in Central City — and rushed her out.

The train was moving. Od handed Berry up to the conductor, and jumped on behind. Berry exclaimed, "Railroads! The fares they charge, you'd think they'd give us time to finish our dinner! Such as it is!"

"Wait till we hit the stageroad south of Trinidad," said Od. "Then, honey, it gets really tough!"

He was a little annoyed with her.

Six horses running, the stagecoach bounced and jolted down the road that was no real road at all, beating up banners of dust that caught up with it and choked the passengers.

The coach, slung high on steerhide thorough-braces, had three seats which nobody in his right mind could expect to accommodate three persons each. Nevertheless, nine paying passengers were crammed inside. The windows were lined with canvas. Opened, they sucked in thick swirls of nose-stinging dust. Closed, the coach became a stifling oven.

Barging across dry riverbeds, the lurch of wheels sinking in sand flung the passengers against one another, then the jar of the opposite bank shook them up and banged their heads on the roof. The driver cracked the whip, his single purpose being to arrive on schedule at the end of his run; neck or nothing and to hell with the passengers. He drew up at a lonely stage-halt, announcing a twenty-minute spell for grub, no more. He had time to make up.

Helped by Od, Berry tottered stiffly out of the coach, sore and starving. This stage-halt was a so-called road ranch, a hangout for stray travelers and saddle tramps who drifted up and down the trail. Od got Berry a seat. The proprietor, who was also the cook, slammed out tin plates of food and collected a dollar on each.

Ravenous, Berry swallowed half-boiled pork and doughy bread that looked as if it had been baked in black ashes. After a chunk of soggy gray pie, washed down with water tasting of alkali, she all at once felt horribly depressed and sick.

She heard the driver bawl out that time was up, but she knew for certain that she couldn't take any more of that horse-drawn hell today. "Can we wait over for the next stage?" she asked Od weakly, and muffled a sour hiccup. "I've got to go to bed." She felt her insides tighten and twist.

She looked sick, Od saw at once. It didn't cross his mind that the poor food, hastily bolted, could be to blame for it. He attributed it to that mysterious female malady unknown to men, and it scared him. He got hold of the proprietor.

"I want a room for the lady. Private. With a decent bed."

"Do you, now?" The proprietor spread his greasy hands on the counter and winked at the listening loafers. "All the best modern conveniences, o' course? Hot and cold water, sewing machine, grand piano, an' the daily papers! I'll notify our head clerk. He's been carefully trained to please the most high-class guests, an' can waltz, make a fourth at euchre, lead in prayer, mind the baby —"

"A room, I said, not a comic recitation!"

The proprietor abandoned his sense of humor. "Hell, man! This ain't no —"

"Name your price."

"Oh. Well, if it's that way." The proprietor provided a room, after hauling three sleeping drunks out of it. "There's no lock," he told Od, "an' some o' these customers —"

"I know."

"Wedge the door, mister, if you don't want to be interrupted."

"Sure," Od said. It was that kind of dive. Waste of breath, any attempt to explain that the young lady was unwell and would sleep alone.

He escorted Berry to the room and backed out, closing the door. He borrowed a rawhide chair and sat outside the door, smoking one cigar after another until late in the night.

The road ranch gradually fell as quiet as the miles of empty land surrounding it, and then he stretched out to sleep uncomfortably on the dirty floor, grinning at himself, thinking, *Od Thornton of the Avalon — nursemaiding a girl! I be damned!*

58

Seldom in her life had Berry suffered from bad dreams. She had learned to thresh out her problems while awake, or at least to see them clearly — as clearly as she could — before brushing them from her mind and going to sleep. Her healthy young body gave her no trouble; she hardly knew she had a stomach.

This night brought a phenomenon compounded from unresolved problems and indigestion.

A tiger stalked her silently through room after room of a great dark house. It was black and gray, and had white eyes. Try as she would, she could not make her fumbling fingers lock a door securely against it. The slinking shape forced open every door before she could find the key. It hooked a paw slyly around the edge of the door, groping for her, and she had to spring back and run on, knowing that she was fast retreating into a hopeless dead-end trap.

In the last room the tiger said, "A little wine?"

It grew to vast size, and it was the fancy mack, and it was also Od Thornton. It strolled confidently forward, cornering her.

She screamed.

Od leaped up and burst into her room. In darkness he searched his way to the bed, not knowing what to expect. His reaching hand touched her. She writhed on the bed, gasping and moaning, the blanket kicked off. He slid his arm under her and raised her up, murmuring, "There, there — there, now, sweetheart! It's all right! There, darling . . ."

She was a terrified girl in the dark, still engulfed in nightmare horror. The pounding of her heart shook her whole body. Od put both his arms around her and held her close. He felt her cling to him tightly, instinct betraying her, and deep tenderness flooded him.

He would not take her down to bawdy Trailtown and the whisky-soaked old Avalon, but to a good life somewhere far removed from all that. Things that he had laughed at now beckoned to him; he wanted them. Most of all, he wanted Berry, wanted her there sharing with him the pleasures and discoveries of that good life which he would build for them both.

Among the snoring drunks in the main room, one of them, sluggishly roused by Berry's moans, shouted a luridly bawdy bit of advice. It raised a laugh from two or three other customers.

It was that, the shout and the laugh, that brought Berry to, like a dash of cold water in the face. But the transition from fading nightmare to waking reality passed so swiftly that she failed to distinguish it.

The aftermath of horror remained. And the fear. Fear of the tiger, the man, confident and overpowering. Fear of herself, the woman, surrendering. From threat she awoke to actuality: in Od Thornton's arms, in her room, on her bed. All her fear turned against him. He had broken in on her in the night. He was the tiger, creeping, pursuing, pouncing.

She struck at him, wrenched free, and hurled herself off the bed on the far side and crouched there. She said, "I'm not going with you! I'm going back!"

After a long silence she heard him swear under his breath. Then he said, "Going back where?"

She couldn't answer that, for she had no place to go and no money to get there, and after another silence Od said, "No — don't quit. You don't have to, I give you my oath."

She saw his dark form straighten up and move to the door. "I won't bother your nightmares again if I can help it," he said, and the door closed quietly and she was alone.

He would have laughed at the joke on himself had she been any other girl.

She crept back into bed. Nightmares? Perhaps. She wanted to believe he'd only been trying to comfort her. But she remembered his arm around her, remembered him looking at her bare flesh, and she knew he was no better than all the rest. She was determined not to sleep, never to sleep in an unlocked room for the remainder of this journey with Od Thornton. She couldn't trust him, nor this raw and savage land of Texas. God knew what awaited her in that unknown town near Red River.

CHAPTER
FOUR

The southbound stage rocked into town, trailing thick dust that burst slowly upward like yellow smoke in the morning sunlight.

Although his regular halt was the office of Tolliver's freight yard, and after that the livery barn for fresh horses, the driver this trip pulled in at the Avalon as a favor.

Od climbed out of the coach and called up to him, "Obliged to you." He turned to help Berry.

Drugged with fatigue, she ignored his arm and stepped blindly out into the gap between the coach and the boardwalk. She would have spilled there and then if he hadn't swiftly caught her. Od set her on her feet, and steadied her.

She pushed his hands away, with tired violence. The dark shadows under her glazed eyes made her face appear startlingly white and thin. Her eyelids drooped uncontrollably. If she saw the Avalon at all, she saw it as one more stage-stop on this interminable journey.

She did see Soft Duval, who had come to the double door of the barroom and now stood regarding her and Od in grave surprise. She crossed the boardwalk to him.

Perhaps from his pale face and neat black suit she drew a blurred impression of respectability. In a plaintive, little-girl voice, like that of a sleepwalker, she said to him, "Please, I want a room. A private room." More distinctly, she added, "With a lock on the door!"

The gambler bowed and offered her his arm, without a word. She took it, and he led her into the Avalon.

The stage driver went so far as to help Od unload Berry's trunk onto the boardwalk. Od invited him in for a drink, but the driver shook his head; some bad business was known to be cooking here in Trailtown and he shied at getting involved. Quite a few people had come out onto the street. The arrival of the strange girl stirred up curiosity and speculation.

Od dragged the trunk inside and went back for his valise. When he entered the barroom and gave it his habitual inspection, it looked just the same as when he had left it eighteen days ago. Cheerlessly clean. Dust cloths still covered the gambling tables, and no foot had marred the dull gleam of the dance floor.

Behind the spotless bar, old George filled a shot-glass, lifted the coffee pot off the spirit lamp and poured coffee black and hot, and stood back, arms folded.

"Morning, George."

"Mornin', Od."

Od sipped coffee and whisky, back and forth, and made them come out even. "Reload, George."

George glanced at his face, and performed the rites again.

Soft Duval came in from the rear. He sat down at his usual table, riffled two packs of cards, and began laying out a forty-thieves tableau.

"I gave her Gloria's old room," he mentioned. "She slammed the door and locked it. I heard her fall in bed. That's one played-out young lady."

"Yeah," Od said.

He gulped the whisky and found he had most of the coffee left. He slid the shot-glass over to George, who reloaded it and gently set the bottle beside it.

"Rode all night in that damned coach. You know how it is, that road. Bounced all night like dice in the box. No sleep."

"Tough on her," allowed Soft. He turned up seven aces on the bottom rows, and frowned slightly. Should have been all eight, of both packs. Getting clumsy. Getting old.

"In fact —" Od emptied his glass and stared at it.

He should not, reason commanded, tell this. Should not confess to a worn-out old bartender and a broken-down gambler.

"In fact," he said, "no sleep to speak of since we left the railroad and took the stage. Don't I look it?" He scrubbed a hand over his whiskers.

"She looked it," Soft said, his lean forefinger sliding the seven aces down to foundation.

"Why didn't you stop a night at some —" George began, and bit off the rest.

Soft Duval swung around deliberately and gazed at George. The gambler's eyes said, as plain as words, *You fat fool, she wanted a room with a lock on the door!*

64

Od drank whisky and chased it with coffee. He said, "She sings. And she dances. She's good."

A feeble statement, but he could do no better. Fatigue caught up with him like a sudden illness, and he knew that Soft and George were growing aware of his turbid state of mind.

"I want to put on a grand new opening, in her honor. Wish we had a stage, like a theater. It's what she's used to. Lights and scenery. Music." He looked the barroom over, and saw it as she would see it. He shut his eyes. "I want a band. I want lights and decorations."

"Well, there's those colored lanterns and ribbons," George reminded him. "The stuff we used when Gloria first came here. I got it stowed away somewhere. As for a band, though — huh!"

"I can rattle the piano some," Soft Duval admitted.

Od shook his head wearily. He thought of Soft's beaten-up partner. "How's the Duke doing?"

"Emma May took him down to Fort Griffin. An army surgeon's tending to him."

"Where'd she raise the money?"

Soft's shrug expressed utter disinterest. His heavy gold watch and chain were missing from his vest. "You better catch some sleep, Od." He turned up the eighth ace. "What's the new girl's name?"

"Berry," Od replied mechanically. From some corner of his mind a small inspiration flickered. "Berry Ripe. She's performed for the crowned heads of Europe, and she's a lady, if anybody asks you. Now I'm going to bed."

"Berry Ripe," Soft murmured. "H'm."

Od paused outside in the rear to gaze somberly along the warped old gallery at that locked door. He hoped she rested well and would sleep the clock around. He hoped that by some miracle she would awaken with better thoughts of him, but he didn't really believe she would.

He heard behind him, in the quiet barroom, George comment, "She didn't strike me as friendly. 'Course, she was tired."

Bunched cards struck the table lightly. Soft never finished a solitaire game. "More than tired, George."

"Something went wrong somewhere along the line, eh?"

"H'm. I can guess what it was!"

The shot-glass and coffee mug plopped into the soapy water of the sink behind the bar. "When she wakes up she'll want a bath, I bet."

"When she sees this goddam layout," said Soft, who rarely cursed, "she'll want to shoot herself!"

"Well, if she's a lady —"

"She locked her door!"

Fully dressed except for hat and boots, Od opened his eyes to gray twilight.

At first the familiar outlines of his room suggested that this was just another morning. Recollection rushed in. He closed his eyes, but his active mind raced about, diligently fitting all the pieces into a tidy whole.

He had slept all day and now it was early evening, not morning. Was *she* awake yet? If she kept herself locked in and silent, what to do about food and a bath?

And her trunk — damn, in the barroom. She would need fresh clothes . . .

The sound of a tentative cough in the room jerked his eyes open again. He lunged out of his bed.

Heze Johns, slumped patiently in a chair, nearly toppled over backward. "Man!" he gulped, recovering himself. "You sure swarm out o' bed in a rush! You got nerves?"

Od sat back on the edge of the bed. He fished for his boots and tugged them on. "Hello, Heze. Waiting long?"

He could have advised Heze that it was unsafe to enter a sleeping man's room and sit still like that, but it wouldn't have done any good. Heze never learned.

Pulling out a silver watch, the town marshal tipped its face to the graying light from the window. "Thirty-seven minutes. But I been comf'table, settin' here."

"Good," Od said, locating his hat. "Find my cigars?"

"Right there on the table." Heze held up a burning butt. "You want one?"

"Not right yet, thank you kindly."

As usual, Heze Johns missed the irony. He settled in the chair and puffed on.

Od remembered that he hadn't asked Soft and George about the Silver Palace. He had taken it for granted that the Silver Palace was shut down by now. Certainly it had looked dead when he passed it this morning on the stage.

He asked Heze, "How'd it go when Judge Parker's marshals rode in? Did the Jims give 'em any trouble?"

Heze Johns shook his head. With the air of imparting glad news, he said, "We ain't had any trouble. The Jims tamed down all of a sudden. Knew I was watching 'em, I guess! No more fights in the Silver Palace. Games closed, and the women wear clothes. The judge ain't had one single reason to send in his U.S. marshals!"

Od hunched forward, elbows on his knees. "I see." He stared down at the darkening floor. This was bad. "Anything else?"

"The Jims have got so tame they've gone into freighting," Heze declared triumphantly. "They've bought out Tolliver — the whole freight yard and line, wagons and all!"

Od nodded. "They got tipped off in time. Got the word that Judge Parker was set to pounce. So they clamp down. Clamp the lid on the Silver Palace. Buy a business. When the storm clears, they're in more solid than ever. They'll throw the Silver Palace wide open again. They'll control the freight business, the supply depot and express station, the saloon trade — they'll have this town by the throat! They'll squeeze it dry!"

Heze Johns thumped to his feet. "I done my best! I put the fear o' —"

"You sat and let the Jims deal themselves a fresh hand! Tamed? Them? They're laughing at you, at me, and at Judge Parker! Now they're businessmen. Solid citizens! Next, they'll open a bank!"

Heze Johns shifted from one foot to the other. "I can't be right every time. No man can. But I swear —"

"Get out!" Od told him. "Get out, you damned fool!"

Heze Johns tramped out, dully alarmed. He had never, in the five years he had known Od, seen him in a rage such as this. Od must be getting nerves, all right. Heze walked off, wagging his head. *He* never got nerves.

Alone, Od sat thinking. He dug a cigar from the box on the table, fired it, smoked fast.

Maybe a chance remained. If the Silver Palace was clamped down, the old Avalon could attract — with Berry . . .

He stalked into the barroom, calling, "George! Any trail outfits camped on the river?"

"Two," George responded, "and four more coming up, I hear."

"Good! Get out those lanterns and ribbons and any other stuff we've got like that, and let's get busy! When the lady wakes up —"

"She's awake. Soft ordered her supper from the Chinaman's."

"Where's her trunk?"

"Soft drug it in to her."

"Oh." Od scratched his bristly jaw and guessed he'd shave and spruce up before doing anything else. "Well, she'll want a bath first."

"Soft's had the bathhouse stove going quite a while," George said. "Plenty hot water."

"And clean towels," put in Soft, from his table. "Fresh mats on the floor, and a scoured-out tub. The Avalon service overlooks nothing. It's the secret of our success and prosperity!" He raised a satiric glance. "Is it tonight, the grand new opening?"

"Hell, no!" Od snapped irritably. "But we've got to work on it."

The gambler nodded. "It'll take some working, all right. I think you brought back the wrong little lady. She's not our kind."

"She won't do!" said George, and Od spun around to face him over the bar.

"What's your meaning? Say it clearer!"

George poured hot coffee. He replaced the pot on the spirit lamp and turned back to Od. "I saw you make this town. I saw you hold it in your fist. It bore your name. You was a rare tough nut in your time."

"In my time?" Od asked, and the gentle slap of Soft Duval's cards ceased.

George chose a shot-glass and uncorked the bourbon. "I mean," he said, filling the glass carefully, "the time when you woulda beat any game or busted hell trying! The time when you never woulda so lost your head as to bank on a bit of a gal to pull —"

"George," Od interrupted him, "I don't think you better say much more along that line."

George lowered his eyes. Then, stretching his credit with Od another notch, he said, "A woman don't do no harm — till a man lets her run his head! Then he's all through, in this business. The higher he flies, the harder he falls. Then he's meat for the undertaker pretty quick." He paused, and added, "Friend Od, you flew high!"

Taking the whisky in one hand and coffee in the other, and raising them in solemn salute, Od said, "Friend George!" He cracked a smile. "You sour

70

bastard. Take it from me, we'll put the Avalon back on top!"

George corked the bottle. "That'll be the day!" he muttered, and Soft Duval inclined his head in silent agreement. They were a couple of worn-out old barroom veterans and their futures hung upon the fortunes of Od Thornton and the Avalon; and upon the success of a scared, unknown bit of a girl who sure didn't belong around a Trailtown saloon.

As she emerged full into the noisy hubbub of the crowd, with all eyes upon her, Berry stopped short. She had learned to conquer stage fright, but this was something else. At first sight this den struck her as a menagerie of weirdly human animals, hairy and unkempt beyond belief, mostly in outlandish garb — enormous spurs and hats, tattered shirts and patched pants, fearsomely strung with revolvers and knives.

Od's hand cupping her elbow urged her on. "Ladies and gentlemen!" Od clarioned. "Your attention, please!"

Berry already had all the attention it was possible to get. She wore her full-length Juliette costume. Maybe, she thought wildly, the more clothes you wore, the more the men liked you. The men's eyes devoured her.

The women's eyes lanced her. They wore little above the nipples, and nothing below the knees. Back East the police would have raided the place and carted them off.

Her mouth dried and her knees trembled. A dance had been going on in the dance hall, left of the barroom, to the jingling of a piano. The piano quit, and those people, too, crowded in to stare at her.

She had learned from Soft Duval that a crowd could be expected for the grand new opening, but nothing like this. The place was packed. With the Silver Palace temporarily tamed down, the men came to see what the extra-special new attraction was that the Avalon had to offer. They were cowmen, trail drivers, with a sprinkling of townsmen and freighters and casual strangers. A lean Mexican in dusty but elegant *charro* garb drank warily alone, a St. Louis drummer clapped his hands loudly, and two stray soldiers, probably deserters, shared a beer.

Most of the spangled women of the Silver Palace had followed the spenders and were in busy circulation, on percentage terms with the bar. A shining queen in a tight silk dress said winningly, "Od, where *have* you been?"

She wore a gold tiara on her blond hair. Od said to her indifferently, "Hello, Gloria," and passed by with Berry.

The colored lanterns and ribbons and flags, though gaily brightening up the place, could not mask out the definite and hoary old personality of the Avalon. Berry's dry throat tightened. She was about to sing in a saloon! A long drop down from splendid dreams of an operatic career. Saloon singer! Od had tricked her, and she hated him for it.

The man was a tiger, precariously controlled by a leash of his own choosing, which he could and would break at any time. He could never really be trusted, she felt, although she wished she didn't.

A thunder of banging feet and slammed glasses greeted Od's preliminary announcement. Od shouted, holding Berry's arm and waving for silence, "Ladies and gents! I have the proud honor tonight to present . . ."

Like a barker for a medicine show, Berry thought, or a blue cootch turn. The brash voice. The dramatic pause, promising lewd delights. For men only.

Yet he pitched the right note for this audience, she had to admit. He had the professional touch, and the confident assurance that so often in her experience seemed to go with reckless courage. She knew that, without his hand on her arm, she would have turned and run. This audience was impossible; she could not hope to please these wild men. Might as well trill arias to apes.

". . . to present, my friends," Od clarioned, "the little lady who has sung and danced — in the famed Royal European Grand Opera — before all the crowned heads of Europe — and won their unstinted plaudits, their finest compliments on her tremendous success!"

More racket of banged feet and glasses, and the genteel drummer clapping his hands.

Berry heard it in a daze. She had never seen a crowned head. The nearest to it was the gold tiara, on the head of that blond bitch, Gloria.

"I introduce," Od proclaimed, "the one and only American — I repeat, *American* — opera star! Miss Berry Ripe!"

The Texas cowboys went wild, applauding with high boot-heels. The women formed a mutually defensive death-watch.

"Miss Berry will now perform her famous Waltz Song!" said Od. He had insisted on that. It was sure-fire.

He led Berry onto the dance floor, let go of her elbow with reluctance, bowed to her, and stepped back.

At the piano Soft Duval sat waiting, his neat black suit well brushed, long-fingered hands poised upward as if in silent benediction. Berry had given him her music and hummed the piece for him several times, and later heard him quietly practicing it. Soft sent her a look of encouragement. For once, an actual smile crept over his pale, aquiline face.

She stood alone in the full-length blue gown and close-fitting bodice and demure little cap sparkling with sequins, surrounded by armed cowboys fresh off the trail. They expected something startling, she was certain — such as throwing off her clothes to prance naked — and she was equally certain they were due to be disappointed. And to her they appeared entirely capable of taking matters into their own hands.

She looked once more at Soft Duval.

The gambler no longer smiled. The message in his eyes told her to be calm, to forget the half-wild trail drivers. In his fashion he was trying to help her regain confidence, telling her she could not fail.

He brought his hands down and struck the piano keys. Following the opening measures, Berry stepped mechanically forward, began singing, and glided into a dance.

It was no good, she knew at once.

The voice was not her own. Her dancing was nervous and unsure. Training and experience informed her that Gounod's Waltz Song required a lilting high-heartedness of expression to bring it off successfully. This thing was wooden, forced. She had been convinced she would fail, and now it was a fact.

The women from the Silver Palace started chattering, satisfied that this kind of competition would never put their lights in the shade. Some of the men drifted back into the barroom, taking women along. Berry caught a glimpse of Od's face, crestfallen and worried; she heard his angry shout: "Quiet, everybody — quiet!"

The blond woman wearing the tiara, whom he had called Gloria, laughed at him. "Now, Od!" She patted his flushed cheek. "Take it easy, and we'll make it a real night yet! Hey — somebody go get the banjo-bangers from the Palace!"

Berry signaled Soft Duval to cut it short. Soft bowed his head, improvised a quick finish, and Berry quit.

The St. Louis drummer asked her what she'd like to drink.

Berry stood staring around. Nobody had ever pulled such a dead flop as this, even in the Victoria Hall at Central City. There, at least, the audience had resorted to outright hostility, had flung pennies. Here in Texas they simply walked off.

Absolute fury flooded up and took hold of her. Savages!

She looked at the drummer, who asked again what she'd like to drink. "Can you do the cakewalk?" she asked him recklessly.

The drummer whipped off his tan derby hat and cradled it in the crook of his left arm. "Girlie, I come from where it come from! Can you?"

"Yes!" Berry said. "I can dance any dance that was ever invented! Mr. Duval? Music, please!"

Soft Duval automatically started in again on Gounod, then managed to fit the Waltz Song into a thumping tempo. Berry lifted her full skirt, flashed her ankles, and strutted.

The drummer, high-stepping with her arm-in-arm, yelled, "That's it, girlie, that's the ticket! You from St. Looey?"

Berry gathered her skirt up higher. She had beautiful legs, and knew it. "I'm Berry Ripe from Bearville!"

The crowd swarmed back in from the barroom, roaring approval, men laughing and exchanging remarks. This little girl had purposely fooled them, leading with low cards like that. She was the real thing. She held aces to spare. The joke was on them.

Soft Duval twisted the Waltz Song trickily all out of shape. At times it got away from him and he vamped along until he could recapture a thread of it.

The pace grew too fast for the drummer. He tossed his derby into the crowd and gasped, "Girlie, you beat me! I'm through!"

Berry grabbed a trail hand by the front of his knotted bandanna. "Come on!" she commanded, and the grinning Texan promptly took up the challenge with what she recognized as a clod-hop, battering the floor with his high boot-heels. He figured he had her on that.

She watched his feet briefly, and proceeded to out-match him.

Her twinkling slippers patted the floor twice to his once. And still Soft Duval struck variations of the Waltz Song. He couldn't get rid of it, but he could do anything required of it. In his deft gambler's hands the piece took on extraordinary flexibility.

To derisive howls from the crowd, the cowboy gave up and withdrew, shaking his head in admiration. "Man! I never —"

"Next!" Berry sang out. At random, she pointed her finger at a big-hatted cattle buyer. "You?"

"Little lady, I can hoe-down all night!"

"Prove it! Mr. Duval — hit it faster! That slow time bores me!"

Her furious energy soon wore out the cattle buyer. Perspiration streaming down his face, he whooshed, "By damn, the drinks are on me!"

The crowd went wild, but Berry wasn't through yet. She swooped at Od. Her eyes glittered at him. "Well?"

Od reached for her hands, and missed. His glowing face reflected his tremendous satisfaction. He gazed at her with possessive pride. "Honey, you showed 'em! You sure —"

She spun around and beckoned to the lone Mexican. "You dance, señor?"

The Mexican swept off his sombrero and bowed deeply, his face lighting up. "You honor me. Yes, I dance a little. But only the Spanish."

She nodded, taking the finger tips that he offered. "Spanish," she called to Soft Duval at the piano, and he at once shifted the Waltz Song into the rippling, slow-seeming, distinctive Spanish tempo.

A hand touched the Mexican on the shoulder, and Od's lean face intruded. "No. Sorry, *amigo*." Od's voice sounded strangely gentle. "This one — this dance is mine."

The Mexican hesitated, examining Od darkly. He shrugged and let Berry go. He stood alone among strangers, *tejanos, americanos*. In Mexico, or even within jumping distance of the border, he would have —

Od swung Berry onto the floor.

The bellowing crowd quieted, watching, prepared now to love anything that Berry might take a whim to do. Berry heard Gloria's voice raised in an attempt at conversation. A dozen men muttered to her to shut up. Berry liked that. She had won the savages over to her. She felt good about it, as long as she didn't think of how she had done it.

In the hush, a heavy wagon could be heard grinding to a halt outside in the street. The sound of the wheels reminded her that this was not necessarily trail's end. That mammoth track ran through, north and south, and people and animals traveled on it. Escape was not entirely hopeless.

Her fear and distrust of Od would not be downed. She flared out her full skirt, dancing with him, and bent her body backward, professionally graceful, to his arm. She felt Od put strength into his arm to support her while they whirled a full circle.

He danced amazingly well. He would never fumble and let her spill away from him. His encircling arm was like iron.

She noticed Soft Duval staring palely at Od. Then she looked at Od. His face glowed again, and his eyes, half closed, gazed down at her in a way that she remembered — hungry and possessive, almost hypnotic.

She looked quickly away.

The face of a new arrival, a tall young man, rose above the outskirts of the dance-hall crowd. It caught Berry's notice because of its startling contrast to other faces around it.

The young man wore no beard or mustache, and his grave face, perfectly smooth and unlined, had a look of marble stability. He looked clean all through, like a boy unspoiled by contact with vice. He had removed his hat, and by a fluke of lamplight his fair hair shone bright gold.

The long lash of a short-stocked whip, looped over his shoulder, struck an incongruous note. If he was a freighter, a teamster, he surely stood far apart from the general run of that cursing, hard drinking, roughneck tribe.

A man waved to him, bawling, "Hi, there, Rothe! Got that short-cut road over the mountains built yet?" The query was evidently a joke. It raised a laugh.

The fair young man shook his head, unsmiling. "Not yet," he answered, and laughter sounded again.

His glance met Berry's, full on, as she danced with Od. He had very clear blue eyes. Berry saw him flush, but whether from anger or shy self-consciousness she couldn't tell. She thought it most likely shyness, and liked him for it. He revived her faith in the existence of some decency among men.

Soft Duval kept watching Od's face. He abruptly brought the dance to an end, and got up from the piano and shoved off into the barroom.

The crowd loosened up. The last dance was an anticlimax, a bit tame after what had preceded it. Colorful, but not a curtain-ringer. Berry detected Od glancing about searchingly, and she guessed he was seeking an idea for a flash wind-up.

She drew free of him and walked straight to the fair young freighter. There still were a few left of nature's noblemen. Or, anyway, one.

Before she could utter a word, Od stood behind her, saying, a tone too solemnly, "Let me introduce Fabe Rothe, the man who moves mountains."

Following that, Od's murmur was strictly for Berry's ear. "If you're not too tired, get this mule to dance with you! Worth a laugh — but watch out for your little toes, honey!"

Berry said, "Hello, Fabe Rothe!"

Fabe Rothe bobbed his fair head, saying something about how he had heard the unusual noise here and got curious and stopped by. Not that he was an Avalon customer; but a busy saloon meant freight and that was his business.

Up close he loomed even taller, and fairer. And just blunderingly awkward enough to save the boyish quality from verging onto adult crudeness. He was perhaps twenty-five, better than six feet tall, splendidly built. Berry marveled at the miracle that had kept his crystal simplicity and innocence intact. He actually didn't know how to behave toward her. He held his hands down at his sides, careful not to touch her.

Soft Duval showed up with a small wine for Berry. For Od, Soft had a double Kentucky, straight, in a water glass.

"Thanks, Soft," Od said, and emptied the glass in two gulps.

Berry sipped the wine. She handed it to Od. "I'm not too tired. Anything to please, I told you! That's what I'm here for, isn't it?"

To Soft Duval she said brightly, "Professor, strike up the band, please! Mr. Rothe and I will dance, by popular request!"

Od gazed at his emptied glass. He worked his mouth, frowning, and turned to Soft Duval. But Soft was walking off to the piano. Od spat and wondered if he was losing his taste; that double shot of bourbon didn't hit his palate just right. But he was all excited inside, of course, and that did queer things to a man's juices.

Berry dragged Fabe Rothe out onto the dance floor, he shaking his head and protesting that he'd never

81

danced in his life and didn't want to. A big laugh welled up. The crowd gathered again.

He was horribly clumsy. His heavy freighter's boots clumped, and his face flamed red and he didn't know what to do with his hands.

"Forget your feet!" she whispered to him. "Just keep looking at *me!*"

Charitably, Soft Duval played in simple waltz time.

Fabe Rothe's dancing improved to a dragging walkaround, and his hands held Berry more firmly. Berry discovered a brightness in his eyes that she had not seen before. He was making a thorough job of looking at her. His face displayed a kind of troubled wonder, while his eyes . . .

For once in her life Berry mistimed a step. Fabe Rothe's boot crushed down on her slipper.

Soft Duval must have observed her wince, for he jingled an abrupt finish.

"Shall we — sit and talk for a while, Mr. Rothe?"

He allowed shakenly that it would suit him. "I'm afraid I'm not much of a talker, though, Miss —"

"My name's Berry."

"Mine's Fabe."

They found a vacant table in the barroom. Od brought Berry her unfinished glass of wine. His blurred eyes made her uneasy, but she said, "No, thank you."

Od frowned at her, at Fabe, and then at the glass. Berry sat very still. Fabe laid his mule-skinner's whip on the table, unaware of anything amiss.

Something wrong worked in Od. He rarely betrayed any effects of drinking, but now he wore the narrow-eyed and intent stare of a man fighting a drunken fog. Broodingly deliberate, he opened his hand, let the wineglass crash to the floor, and walked away.

Berry breathed again. She saw Soft Duval scanning Od sharply, expectantly.

Fabe Rothe spread his elbows on the table and leaned forward. He said seriously, as though in answer to a spoken question, "I'm a kind of wildcat freighter. I own my outfit, clear — wagon and trailer, and fourteen of the best mules you ever saw. It's right outside. Maybe you'd like to see it?"

He reminded her of a boy in school. "Perhaps later on," she told him.

Od would not, she felt positive, let her out of his sight tonight for a minute. He watched her, his back to the crowded bar. He was not drinking, yet his eyes were slits and now his face grayed over, gaunt and unhealthy, ugly, hardly recognizable.

Gloria went and asked Od something, standing directly before him. Od reached a hand out slowly and pushed her aside. Gloria's raised voice reached Berry.

"What ails you, Od? You look bad, like you're sick!"

Gloria glanced around at the nearest men. They shook their heads. One, the cattle buyer who had danced with Berry, shoved in alongside Od and spoke to him.

Od gave no sign of hearing him; he would not break off his steady stare at Berry. The cattle buyer sent a look at Berry and went on talking, putting his face closer to Od's ear.

Berry said to Fabe, "So you own your own business. Is it successful?"

She had to keep talking, keep him from leaving her. There at the bar Od watched, waiting, in that weirdly menacing mood.

Fabe replied honestly, "Well — yes and no. I was doing well enough, freighting from the railhead to Quemado. I got along with Tolliver. We had an understanding. Then he sold out to the Jims. I don't get along with them. They offer me trouble."

"Why?"

"They want my route. That's all." Fabe leaned back in his chair. "I'd sell out to the Jims," he said, "if they'd give me the right kind of money."

The cattle buyer talked insistently into Od's ear. He flattened out a hand expressively. Three or four men nodded approval, and leveled cold looks at Fabe. They were cowmen, Texans. Fabe Rothe was a freighter, a hobnailed Dutchman from Iowa or somewhere.

The cattle buyer won part of Od's attention at last. Od lifted his lowering head, and his chest heaved, though his eyes stayed on Berry.

"What would you do with the money, Fabe?"

Placing a forefinger on the table, Fabe drew an imaginary map. "It's a good ten days' haul from the railhead to Quemado, because you got to swing way down round the mountains to get there, through Mockingbird Gap and up again, like a hook. I mean the mountains over there, west."

He motioned, indicating that the mountains lay just across the table.

84

"Quemado is the coming town over there. Army building new posts, and settlers pouring in. Railroad builds so slow, take it a hundred years to get down here — and another hundred years to push on over there round the mountains. Long as I live, that means freight to Quemado! Wagons and mules! But they've got to do it faster! You see?"

"Yes," Berry murmured. She watched Fabe's finger, steadfastly avoiding Od's staring eyes. "Yes, of course. But if you sold out —"

"I know a short-cut through the mountains. Right there!" Fabe scored his finger across the imaginary mountains on the table. "Needs work on it. They all laughed at me about it, but I know I could cut three days off that roundabout route to Quemado. I'd build that short-cut road through the mountains, and then they'd be only too glad to use it. Quemado is going to need a lot of freight."

"But what would you get out of it?"

"I'd charge everybody a tariff to use my road."

"A toll road!" Berry exclaimed. It appealed to that practical side of her that stubbornly clung to solid values. She had struggled too long with insecurity. Fabe's idea, aimed at a safe and sure livelihood, struck her as sheer genius. "Why, I think that's wonderful!"

He smiled at her across the table. "There'd be plenty of traffic. I expect the stage line would —"

"Of course! Then you could build a stage-stop! And serve meals!"

She almost forgot Od, until from the corner of her eye she saw him shrug heavily and bob his head.

The cattle buyer stepped back, satisfied. He motioned to another man, a trail boss, and came striding toward the table.

Berry said to Fabe, "You'd better go now!"

His smile faded. He blinked slowly at her, perplexed. "What's wrong?" He picked up his whip. "What did I say wrong?"

Followed closely by the trail boss, the cattle buyer came up alongside Fabe. "Little lady, he's bothered you way too much!" he remarked kindly. "Move, mule-skinner!" He kicked the chair out from under Fabe and jabbed an elbow hard at his face. "The lady's had enough o' you!"

Fabe flew backward, all arms and legs. His fall shook the floor, and the rungs of the chair snapped under him. His legs flailed up and over in a somersault that landed him some distance from the table. The cattle buyer boomed a laugh, doffing his hat to Berry.

"Now, Mr. Schroeder, I ask you!" said the trail boss in mock complaint. "What did you need me for?"

"To hold my coat, Mr. Perry! Only I plumb forgot to —"

That was as far as the cattle buyer got, because the whiplash snaked tight around his neck and strangled off the rest.

Fabe, blood spurting from his nose, jerked the whip. He had flung the lash accurately while bounding to his feet. Half dazed, he moved from a freighter's first impulse to use the tool he knew best.

He hauled the cattle buyer in, floundering, and struck him once with his massive left fist. He tried to twirl the lash free then, to use again, but the slumping man's chin held it.

The trail boss charged at him, arms spread and fists bunched. Fabe kicked him in the foremost knee. Squinching his face, the trail boss sprawled forward.

Fabe kicked him again. He wrenched his whip loose. His glaring eyes lighted on Od, who was pacing forward, frowning.

The heavy whip whined. It struck the leather tops of Od's high boots, which he wore underneath his trousers, and curled around. But the end of the thong whisked higher and bit viciously into the calf of Od's leg.

The pain snapped Od out of his fog. He snatched down at the lash, caught it. He went hand-over-hand along the lash, like a cowboy to a roped steer.

Fabe swung that left fist at him, missed, lost balance, and Od elbowed him off and tore the whip away from him. The thick butt of the whip was of plaited rawhide, hard as iron. Od slammed it down on Fabe's head, twice. It sounded like an ax whacking into a tree on a frosty morning.

"You rotten animal! You killer!"

On her knees beside Fabe, Berry stared up at Od. Fabe, on the floor, breathed harshly through his gaping mouth, eyes closed.

"You tried to murder him!"

Od shook his head down at her. "No, I didn't want —" he began vaguely, and lost the sense of what he meant to say.

Smart pain up the back of his leg irritated him. "Take care of that fool," he said to the crowd. He let the whip fall, and trod back to the bar.

Soft Duval said, "Let's get this boy on his wagon and start him off."

"He can't drive!" Berry cried at him. "He's hurt! He —"

The gambler's calm eyes commanded her to silence. His voice said, "He'll be all right. Got a thick skull. His mules know the road."

Some of the men lifted Fabe up. They showed no concern, and even made jokes about him. They carried Fabe out of the Avalon, the front way, to his freighting outfit. Just a dumb mule-skinner who had pushed out of turn and got smacked down.

In the mild commotion of carrying Fabe out, Soft Duval muttered to Berry, "Slip out the back, like you're going to your room for a minute. Come round to the front. Take your time. I'll be at Rothe's freight wagon. I'll get shed of the others."

Soft Duval was waiting for Berry when she came hurrying around the Avalon.

The size of Fabe's outfit astonished Berry. A huge wagon, square-sided. A trailer of the same size and shape hitched behind. Ahead, spans of big mules in harness. A shape lay spread out atop the tarpaulin covering the wagon. A man's shape.

On the driver's seat, holding the lines, Soft Duval said, "Climb up here."

88

She climbed up beside him, and he said, "You want out of this. All right, I know. I'll get your trunk out tomorrow and ship it on. Take the lines. Here! Just hold them. The mules know the road."

She shivered. "This is crazy. Od will come after me!"

The gambler's pale eyes gleamed at her in the glow from the front windows of the Avalon. "I dropped something in his double Kentucky, half an hour ago. He should be out before now, but he's tough. He'll be out soon, don't worry. He can't last much longer."

She took the lines. Soft Duval lowered himself down over the wheel on his side, saying, "That joker" — nodding back to the shape spread on the tarpaulin — "won't hurt you. He's pure as a lamb. Wait for me in Quemado!"

On the ground, he took off his hat and walked forward to the lead span of mules. He swung around, eyes still gleaming, and called to her gently, "Quemado, honey! Wait there for me!"

He hit the lead span with his hat, and waved to her as she lurched past on the driver's seat. "Quemado!"

The double freight wagon lumbered out of town, strained harness creaking and the great wheels thumping the ruts.

Hat in hand, Soft Duval stood watching it go. He was getting along in years, but he didn't feel old tonight; he hoped she didn't regard him as old. And he felt he was doing a double favor — for himself and for Od Thornton.

He became aware of two horsemen trotting quietly past, riding in the dusty wake of the freight wagon.

They kept to the far side of the street, but enough light touched them from the Avalon's front windows to show him who they were: Tom Brien and another Jims' man, name of Harve.

"Where headed?" he hailed them, knowing where and for what purpose. The Jims were bound to crack down on Fabe Rothe. They had sunk a small fortune, buying Tolliver's freighting business, and would not tolerate any wildcat trade competition. The two men must have been waiting for Rothe to come out of the Avalon. It was just bad luck that they should pick this night.

The two riders reined in sharply. Harve, a man of quick temper, made to come on over to Soft Duval. Tom Brien muttered a restraining word to him, and called to Soft, "Any o' your affair, tinhorn?"

"Why, yes," Soft Duval responded mildly. "I want that wagon to get through to Quemado. I don't want something happening to it — not this trip, anyhow. You better turn back."

"The hell! For you?"

Soft Duval sighed, wishing he hadn't slipped the knockout drops into the stiff drink he had handed Od at the end of the dance. It had seemed the best thing to do then. Better than having to sneak-shoot Od to get Berry away from him. After all, Od was his friend. But he needed Od now.

"You better turn back," he repeated. His tone made it a flat command.

"Goddam!" grunted Harve. His gun roared a streak, while Tom Brien yelled at him to keep his head.

90

Soft Duval sleeved out a two-shot derringer and ran at them. The stubby derringer was chancy at longer range than about fifteen feet, and the light was bad. His first shot took Harve somewhere near the belt, and the second load went wasted because he stumbled.

Harve slid off his horse on its blind side, holding onto the reins, and fired under its belly. The horse refused to stand for that and reared off, uncovering Harve and tugging at the reins.

Lying in the street, Soft dropped his empty pistol and plucked out its mate. He cocked it, shoved it out to arm's length, fired, and got Harve again. Harve fell, letting his horse go. Soft slid his outstretched arm in the dirt, trying for aim at Tom Brien, but his finger tightened too soon and the shot blasted sand and dust.

Tom Brien quit yelling and slashed gunfire at Soft. His horse bowed up and plunged in a mad circle, so that Tom Brien fired first from one side and then the other.

Od reeled out of the Avalon, banging the double doors wide open on their hinges. He saw Soft Duval's crumpled body, and he loosed a shot at Tom Brien. His bullet slapped the painted sign of the livery across the street. Tom Brien, bouncing high, blazed once at him and tried to get his spooked horse straightened out.

Foggily annoyed, Od steadied his gun, using both hands. He cut down on Tom Brien and worked the trigger fast. The gun spat like a Hotchkiss. Tom Brien jolted out of his saddle. The horse careened off, lashing its heels at shadows.

Very deliberately, Od stepped across the boardwalk, making for Soft Duval. At the edge of the boardwalk his foot found nothing and he pitched headlong into the street, and then he was all through.

Marshal Heze Johns, pushing through the gathered crowd a minute later, looked the situation over. "My Lord! Four dead! A shoot-out — and Judge Parker and Bowers only waiting to jump in. Now there's real hell to pay!"

CHAPTER
FIVE

Od woke up feeling as if he had been sick for a long time.

His first glance told him that he was in a room of the Todd Hotel. A smell of perfume informed him it was a woman's room. He shut his eyes again. His head ached violently.

Gloria said, some time later and stroking his head with her finger tips, "Honey, somebody slipped nasty ol' knockout drops in your drink. You've been dead to the world since night before last. Now, you take it easy. You're sick!"

"What's gone on?"

"Oh, nothing much since the shooting. But those damned marshals are in town. Judge Parker's marshals. Honey, they're looking for you!"

Od sat up in the bed. A dizzy spell took him and he broke out in a cold sweat while fighting for control of his sour stomach.

When he could risk opening his mouth, he asked Gloria, "Ray Bowers?"

She held him steady in her arms, letting her bright yellow hair brush against his dark mop. "Yes, Bowers is leading the hunt for you. They're pretty certain you didn't skip town. Nobody knows where you are, though, except old George. A couple of trail hands helped carry you here, but they've left with their outfit."

He made to get up, muttering his need to wash and dress.

Gloria wouldn't let him. "No you don't! You've got the shakes too bad. I'll go get George to fix you one of his morning specials."

"All right. Tell him to make it double."

When she returned, though, Od had made use of the corner washstand and was getting dressed. He combed his hair at her dressing table, she watching him with a sulky frown. "Here's the bottle and a glass," she said. "And George sent your razor."

He shook his head, immediately regretting it because of pain stabbing across his eyes. "No shave today. I'd slice my ears off."

Wryly he peered at his reflection in the mirror. His face looked haggard and, due to the sprouting stubble, darker than usual — and older. The eyes, puffed and bloodshot, were like those of a chronic drunkard.

"Somebody," he observed, "sure fixed me!"

"George can tell you who did it," Gloria said.

He turned and looked at her carefully, detecting for the first time the ill-humor that had come over her. It occurred to him that he had neglected to thank her for hiding him in her room.

Then the thought came that he was not only in her debt, but in her hands. He would have to treat her with caution. Gloria in good humor was great fun; in a bad temper she was something else. Her loyalty had limits, as she had proved when she quit the failing Avalon and went over to the rival Silver Palace for better money.

Od drank some of George's morning special, a concoction of peculiar odor and color. He had some trouble holding it down, and Gloria asked, "Does it taste as bad as it looks?"

"Bad enough to cure anything," he replied.

The stuff did have some kind of hidden merit, because he began feeling better and was able to finish the bottle. Gloria sat on the edge of the bed, tapping a toe, and he suddenly went to her and kissed her.

It caught her by surprise, but her response was instant. She gripped him fiercely, her fingers digging into his back, her lips pressed hard on his.

In a moment he freed himself from her, saying, "That shooting is on my mind. All I know is, Tom Brien was emptying his gun into Soft Duval — so I shot him."

She smoothed her hair, gazing at him strangely.

That much, she told him, was about all anybody else knew. Soft Duval and Tom Brien and Harve were dead. The main thing now was, the gun battle had brought on an invasion by U.S. Marshal Bowers and a mob of his deputies.

"He doesn't like you, honey, does he?" observed Gloria.

"No more than I like him," Od agreed. "What's he doing now?"

"He's posted men all around the town with rifles, and swears he'll find you if he has to rip the town apart.

That's a big order. Anyway, they can't come busting in *my* room!"

Gloria seemed to think, if she gave it any thought at all, that the whole thing would somehow blow over.

Od knew better. He was in a bad tight. The more he studied it the worse it got. Bowers had orders from Judge Parker to crack down on Trailtown at the first chance, and the gun battle offered that chance. Ray Bowers finally had Od well on the hook, and he'd never go back empty-handed to the judge.

By prodding Gloria along and keeping her to the subject, Od learned that Tom Brien's friends in the Jims' crew also were on the lookout for him. "How about Heze Johns?" he asked her.

She shrugged impatiently. "He don't amount to beans now. When he tried to act important, Bowers called him a damned nuisance and shoved him away. He was in his shack when I passed, looking like a kid trying not to bawl."

"I want to see him," Od said, his mind racing, searching. "Do me a favor and go tell him to come up here."

She widened her blue eyes. "Heze Johns? You've lost your mind, Od! I'd never trust the fool! He might yell for Bowers!"

"No, he won't. You say Bowers handled him rough and made small of him. That makes a difference, if I know Heze. Go get him."

"I won't!" she flared at him. "You sit down and stop talking — little Gloria is boss in this room!"

"Thanks for everything," he murmured. He picked up his hat and left.

From the hotel to the town marshal's office it was some forty long strides, and Od took them fast.

A glance showed him that Bowers's deputies were swinging into an organized search of the town. The main street was alive with men, mostly onlookers hurrying from one point to another after the armed searchers, all anxious to be in at the capture — or the kill.

The busiest spots were the freight yard, the livery barn, and the warehouse of Bateman's Grocery & General Merchandise. And that indicated the type of mind that Bowers had: a thinking mind, professional. An unthinking amateur might have looked first in the best bed of the hotel, instead of digging into dark corners for the wanted fugitive.

Od wondered for a moment if he was actually going to reach the town marshal's office unnoticed among the crowd. He got more than halfway there before somebody called to him, "Hey!" And then on a rising shout of astonishment, "*Hey!*"

Od strode on swiftly without turning his head. He stepped into the bare little office, throwing the door shut behind him.

Heze Johns jumped up behind his desk, knocking his old Douglas chair askew and blinking, too confused to take off his reading glasses. He started to blurt out the first question that came into his head. "How in —"

Od cut him off. "Listen! I hear I'm wanted on a murder charge. All right, I'm surrendering to you. To you! Not to Bowers. Get it?"

"Me?"

"Dammit, Heze, use your head quick for once! We don't have much time!" Od listened to the swelling noise outside, the rumble of excited voices, the clacking boot-heels. A man snapped a question, received replies, and followed with a quiet command. That was Bowers.

Feet trotted briskly past the thin wooden side-walls, to the rear. It took the deputies only a few seconds to surround Heze Johns's little shack of an office. And there stood Heze blinking through his glasses, too slow to grasp the situation. Od stepped around the desk and stood beside Heze, keeping Heze between himself and the window. He drew his gun and laid it on the desk, and covered it with his hat.

"Heze, I'm your prisoner. You've arrested me. I give up my gun to you — but leave it there! Bowers is outside. You better tell him to come in."

Heze Johns called out obediently, "Mr. Bowers, you can come in!"

The head marshal opened the door unhurriedly and came in a step, alone. "I was just about to, *Mister* Johns," he drawled, with obvious contempt for Heze. He nodded to Od. "I'll take your gun, Thornton! I arrest you on the charge of murdering Tom Brien!"

Od fingered his coat open to show the empty holster. "I'm already under arrest. I've surrendered to Johns. You're too late, Bowers."

Ray Bowers's face was crinkled as if the flesh had shrunk from too much riding into the dry wind and sand and scorching sun, leaving the skin to find its own fit like a rider's goatskin glove. He smiled. The smile was a measure of his anger, and the skin became crushed into a thousand sharply angular little furrows and ridges. His eyes were round and black, very small in that great hairless wreck of a face.

"So you surrendered," he said, still smiling. "You knew I had this town ringed in. You knew you didn't have a chance in the world to get away from me. So you surrendered to Johns. It won't do you a bit of good in Judge Parker's court, if that's what you hope!"

"What you mean is," Od said, "I can't hope for a fair shake in court — if you can help it!"

That remark wiped off the smile. "I've never given false witness against any man," Bowers stated quietly. "I never in my life lied under oath, if that's what *you* mean! You better come along. Johns can't hold you. He's only town marshal, for one thing."

Od placed his hands on the desk and bent forward. "It happens Johns has also got a deputy sheriff's badge."

"Special deputy sheriff, unpaid," Bowers corrected. "I know. They're ladled out by the dozen, these days. Any town marshal can get one for the asking. To me they don't count. Come along, I said!"

Having his armed deputies ready outside, he had dropped his gun back into its holster. He patted the butt as a gesture to enforce his command. "No more talk!"

99

As if to comply, Od picked up his hat with his left hand. "A local peace officer doesn't count with you? You're a government officer, a big man! You shove a mere Texas lawman, and take away his prisoner. Like in reconstruction days, h'm? I wonder how our state governor will appreciate it, seeing it was him called in federal law officers! It'll put him in a jam with Texas voters. He'll have to wriggle out of that — most likely at the cost of a certain federal officer's scalp!"

Ray Bowers gazed at the desk, at Od's uncovered gun and right hand resting an inch from it. He raised his round black eyes and scanned Od's face. "Your local peace officer is careless! He should pick that gun up and make good on the arrest!"

Od moved back, letting Heze take the gun, and Bowers said next, "Mr. Johns, I agree he's your prisoner. I suggest he be handcuffed till you deliver him at Tascosa, on the mail-stage. Let's not get careless again!"

"I'm never careless!" Heze retorted. "Never! Handcuffs? Let's see, I had a pair somewhere around. Lost the key, though, so they wouldn't be much good."

Ray Bowers's face became as crumpled as a huge wad of brown paper. He was smiling again, at Od.

"Don't get any hopes up, Thornton," he said ever so softly. "We're *all* going to Tascosa. We'll all ride with the mail-stage, for company. Mr. Johns, you may use my handcuffs on your prisoner. I'll keep the key!"

★   ★   ★

All Trailtown, it appeared to Od, turned out to see him off on what appeared to be generally regarded as his last journey.

The two Jims stood with a group of their men from the Silver Palace and the freight yard, Jim Bloud laughing and talking, his heavy double-chin bulging when he turned his head to speak to his partner.

Jim Kerry, unsmiling, didn't respond to Jim Bloud. He seldom responded to anybody. His eyes, mouth, and chin ran parallel horizontal lines across a face shaped like a keystone. As far as anybody knew, Jim Kerry never found humor in anything, even the downfall of an enemy.

Soon, Jim Kerry walked off indifferently, while Jim Bloud bellowed a joke that had to do with hanging.

Ray Bowers had slipped leg irons on Od as well as the handcuffs. Heze helped Od into the coach and climbed in after him, his manner a mixture of importance and apology.

While Bowers conferred with the driver, George and Gloria came over and talked with Od through the coach windows.

Leaving the driver, Bowers strode around the coach and demanded, "What's this? What are you two up to?"

"Talking business with the boss," George grunted, and went on to tell Od that he had locked up the Avalon until things quieted down. "I'll pack your valise and send it on to you," he added gloomily.

"And I'll send you something to eat," Gloria promised, close to tears. "That jail food's lousy, they tell me. Here's your razor that you left behind, honey."

"Whoa! I'll take that weapon!" Bowers reached a long arm over her shoulder and plucked the razor from her hand.

Gloria spun around and took a healthy smack at him. Bowers guarded it off, smiling coldly while he put two and two together.

"So that's where he was hiding out. With you! In your hotel room?"

One of the younger deputies exclaimed disgustedly, "Beat that! And us workin' like dogs, rootin' through that warehouse!"

"Lady, let me help you into the coach," Bowers urged, with a politeness that was more chilling than any angry outburst. "The judge will talk some law to you!"

"What?" Gloria screamed. "Me travel in these clothes?"

"They look all right to me, and the judge won't care." Bowers patted George's hip pocket and relieved him of his short-barreled .44. "I guess you're mixed in it, too. Hop in, both of you!"

They raised an impressive flurry, the prisoner-laden mail-stage with Bowers's armed deputies trooping alongside, clattering out of Trailtown.

Because of Gloria's loud wrath and George's bitter silence, it was some time before Od could bring up the subject that had been itching his mind ever since he came to in Gloria's room. "How's Miss Berry taking all this?"

George stared blankly at him and then at Gloria. "Didn't you tell him?" he asked her.

Gloria shook her head, and George said, "Why, she's been gone since night 'fore last, man! Hey — hold it!"

Od lunged at the coach door with his manacled hands, with a wild idea of ordering the driver to turn back. A tough young deputy riding alongside brought his rifle around. Od sank slowly back on his seat, looking at nothing.

He heard George saying, "I saw her leave the barroom just before the shooting started. She never came back. Some think she caught a ride with that mule-skinner, Rothe. Didn't take her trunk or anything, but she sure left town. She's sure gone!"

In any case involving a major crime, Judge Solomon Parker's habit was to hold an informal hearing in an office of the stone courthouse, without lawyers.

He would let the accused and the accusers argue while he sat combing his beard, then raise a commanding hand, speak a few words, and that closed the hearing. By the tone of his remark the eventual fate of the prisoner could be predicted.

A newspaper had referred to him as King Solomon. The judge framed the clipping, and his record that session was seventeen men sent to the gallows.

Slowly blinking his pale, watery eyes, Judge Parker listened to U.S. Marshal Bowers tell of three men killed in a gun battle outside the Avalon in notorious Trailtown.

The judge's glance ranged over the unshaven prisoner in manacles, and on to George, to Heze Johns, and lastly to Gloria. His hand crept up to his white beard, and he shifted in his chair and belched.

Summing up briefly, Bowers said, "It was a saloon feud. The gambler, Duval, jumped the two Silver Palace men, and Thornton helped shoot them down. Duval got killed. Thornton got clear. The woman hid him, kept him hid even when she knew he was a wanted fugitive. This feller is a bartender of his, and knew about it — may have been mixed in the shooting, too. This other man is the town marshal. Thornton made a play of surrendering to him, after he knew it was all up. Judge, that's about all."

The judge raised his hand, prepared to pronounce a few words. Evidently recollecting that the prisoner had not yet spoken, he lowered his hand and sent Od a grudging nod.

Instead of speaking, Od let George take the floor. During the latter part of the journey he had roused himself and gone into deep conference with George and Gloria, and with Heze Johns.

George tugged his vest straight and took off his derby hat. "It was Soft Duval," he began in his grumbling, unhappy way. "Rest his soul, Soft was a good ol' wagon, but he had a bad streak. He wanted a crack at the Silver Palace bunch for what they done to a friend o' his. Ev'body knows about that. But he knew Od wouldn't stand for any gunplay, any more'n the town marshal. So he drugged Od that night, then made his play. I saw him lace a double whisky with knockout drops."

"Why didn't you stop him?" Bowers demanded skeptically.

George rolled a stout shoulder. "Too busy. Didn't know who it was for, anyhow, till I saw Od drink it. When the shooting started, Od was awful groggy, but still on his feet. He rocked out to stop the fight."

"And he shot Tom Brien!"

"No," said George. "He shot Duval. But by then Duval had killed Harve *and* Tom Brien. Then Od passed out cold."

"Passed out is right!" put in Gloria. "Took four of us to carry him up to my bed. He was out dead for a day and a half." She reflected, and added, "Naturally, I slept in another room."

"Oh, naturally!" Bowers snarled, his smile threatening to crack his dry skin into pieces. "You Trailtown folks are purer than —"

Od nudged Heze Johns, and Heze burst out, "Od was laying there in the street like a corpse, like the others! Gun smoking in his hand! I said, 'Lord, ain't it hell he's dead!' Right, George?"

"No, you said, 'My Lord, looks like they're all dead an' hell to pay!' I think that was it. Half the town heard you."

The judge raised his slab face and regarded Od more closely.

"Well," Heze said soberly, "a man don't know. I was upset. Od always backed me up in law and order. I thought sure they'd finally got him — the Silver Palace bunch. He looked dead to me." He was stolidly sincere about it, and convincing.

The judge stopped combing his beard, and his commanding hand stayed passive on his paunch. King Solomon was re-weighing his unspoken decision, for within the limits of his grim conception of justice he was incorruptibly just. A man had crimed or he had not crimed. No middle ground existed. There was no such thing as second-degree murder. It was murder, or it was nothing, and on the uncompromising blade-edge of Parker's judgment the man went free or went to hell.

Bowers turned on Od. "What's this you're trying to pull on me, Thornton?"

Od spread his manacled hands. "I haven't opened my mouth. I will, though, now you invite me."

He inclined his head respectfully to Judge Parker. "With your permission, sir."

The judge shifted his hefty bulk again, belched again. His chalky eyes lifted and took wandering aim at the ceiling.

"Thank you, sir!" Od faced Bowers. "You say I was hiding from the law, and that I finally gave up only because I had to. That's a lie!"

He wanted to break Bowers's chill composure. He was fighting with every trick at his command. "I was right there at the hotel, sleeping off the drug. As soon as I came to —"

"You —" began Bowers, but Od let his voice rise and crackle.

"I walked openly out of the hotel and up the street in broad daylight to the town marshal's office, where I voluntarily surrendered to Johns — as he'll bear witness! You were searching the whole town for me? So you say! It sounds more as if you were running in circles, looking for a scapegoat!"

"You —" tried Bowers again.

"When you heard that somebody had surrendered to the town marshal," Od pursued, "what did you do? You moved in to grab the credit for an arrest! Didn't you try to take me away from Johns? Tell the truth!"

At last Bowers lost his temper. He shouted to Judge Parker, "This man is twisting the facts and making me out a liar! He's a gambler and saloon owner, and — and —" He swung around and pushed his face close to Od's. "Thornton, I hate your guts and —"

"I know you do," Od said, and now his voice was mild and reasonable. "Why else would you drag me all the way here on a trumped-up charge?" He pulled his head back then, because for a moment Bowers appeared about to smash a fist at him.

The judge splayed his fingers and patted his paunch, and spoke to the marshal. "The charge against this man is murder. His occupation is not our concern. He hasn't denied taking part in the shooting, but it seems probable that he shot at the one who started it — the one who put the drug in his drink."

He paused, and brought out ponderously, "The circumstances attending his action place the said action in a category removed from murder. And evidently he did surrender himself to the local peace officer, when he was able, while you were supposedly ransacking the town for him!"

"Yes, but it was one of those crazy things that —"

"Marshal, I fear you were negligent on the one side, and over-zealous on the other!" the judge rebuked him, raising his hand. "Your personal dislike of this man may be quite justified, but I feel that you do not have a good case against him. You may as well let him go, and trust to better luck next time."

Outside, while unlocking the manacles, Bowers breathed, "Next time, yes!" His face had a grayish-brown hue. "Next time, Thornton, I'll get you right!"

In Trailtown, Od received the impression that his free return was regarded as a miracle. Men crowded into the Avalon to shake his hand and swear they had been pulling for him.

Ted Sieker came over from the livery stable with a flat package for Od, explaining that he had picked it up in the mail for him.

"Golly, Od, it's good to see you back!" young Ted exclaimed. "I guess they're right — you must have something on Judge Parker!"

"Oh, sure," Od said, knifing open the package. "We're old partners in crime. What's this? Money!"

There was a note wrapped around the sheaf of banknotes, scrawled in a round hand, in pencil. Od's knife had cut through it. He pieced the note together, and read: *This repays the $1000 you advanced me in Central City. Fabe has sold the freight business and we will build the toll road. We are married. Please care for my trunk until I can send for it. Thank you. — Berry (Mrs. F. Rothe).*

108

That evening the Avalon boomed, wide open and roaring. The gambling room ran full blast and the dance floor was crowded. All the women from the Silver Palace flocked in, following the fast money. They said the Silver Palace was on the skids; the Jims had clamped the lid on and blighted that place.

Although kept on the jump, George found time to speak to Gloria about Od. "All the time I've known him," George said worriedly, "I never seen him drink like this. What's got into him? He ain't sociable."

"That's for sure!" said Gloria. She had tried to sweeten Od out of his black mood, and got a blank stare.

"He looks ugly. If he gets in trouble again, you know where it'll land him! Bowers will —"

"I know it as well as you do."

"Well — can't you do nothin' with him?"

"Not while he's got that singing girl on his mind," Gloria snapped sorely. "I can't sing a damn note!"

CHAPTER
SIX

Wiping her perspiring face on her apron, Berry left the tiny kitchen and walked through the main room to the open front door. She stood there fanning herself with the apron, watching for Fabe and Tolliver to return from inspecting the toll road. Much depended upon Tolliver's verdict.

She could see nothing but the rock slopes and towering crags, dull black and forbiddingly lifeless. The mountain pass at this highest point was narrow and crooked, as effective as giant prison walls in shutting out all sight of the outside world.

Fabe had judged it the best location for the toll station. It contained a spring of good water, and some flat places that made natural pens for horses and mules, with very little fencing required. Fabe favored economy and convenience far above scenery. It didn't bother him that the only sound at night was the eerie howl of some distant coyote. He slept like a log.

From here the toll road itself was invisible to Berry, but she knew its look well, for she had helped Fabe work on it after he ran out of money and had to let go his hired Mexican laborers. It snaked along three tortuous miles of ledge high above the canyon, timber-braced here and there, the narrowest spots bridged with pine and cottonwood logs hauled up nine miles from the forest this side of Quemado, west. She had never known such savagely heartbreaking work.

She heard the two men coming up the road, and hastened back in to set out their dinner. Fabe hated waiting, hated to waste time. And she had taken especial pains over the meal, to please Tolliver, on whom so much depended.

Tolliver entered the toll station with Fabe, saying, "I tell you, that's one hell of a road! You got to do more work on that last grade. A loaded wagon could slide off down the canyon. I wouldn't risk it."

"I'll fix that," Fabe said, and Berry caught the worry in his voice. Fabe was over-anxious.

Berry served dinner, herself last. The two men were eating before she sat down. Tolliver passed some compliments on the food, and Berry thanked him. He was a decent enough kind of man, though a hard trader, a tough business adventurer.

It was Tolliver who had bought Fabe's freight outfit. He was buying other wildcat outfits, too, and already had a string of them. He claimed that the Jims had pressured him to sell his Trailtown business to them, and he was vengeful. He was out to establish a new freight line from railhead to Quemado, using Fabe's toll road if feasible, and beat out the Jims.

"Tell you what, Rothe," he said, pushing away his empty plate and filling his pipe. "God help me, I'll use your road! I guess your wife's good food has mellowed me."

He fired up his pipe, giving Berry time to flash an eager smile at Fabe, who didn't respond to it.

"You'll never regret it," Fabe assured Tolliver, too quickly. "It'll cut nearly half the time off the old long road. Ten dollars a wagon is —"

"Too much," Tolliver broke in affably. "Five is about right. My crews will stop here to eat, and you'll make some profit on that. Of course, I don't expect you to let the Jims haul over this route. We better put that in writing."

He narrowed his sharp eyes a trifle, and added, "I'll put up a hundred dollars right now to seal the contract, if it suits you."

"It suits me!" Fabe said, ignoring Berry's warning shake of her head.

Tolliver counted out the money and shook hands with Fabe on it. Knowing that he had driven a hard bargain, and not missing Berry's head-shake, he promptly changed the subject. "What d'you think of the news from Trailtown, Miz Rothe?"

"No news reaches us up here, Mr. Tolliver," Berry told him. "I'm looking forward to when our road will be traveled. What news do you mean?"

"Od Thornton got pulled in for killing Tom Brien. Soft Duval and another feller got killed in the same shootout. 'Course, that's nothing special for Trailtown, but here's the thing — Judge Parker turned Thornton loose without even a trial!"

"Too bad!" Fabe observed. His scalp, under his blond hair, bore a scar from Od's knocking him senseless with the stock of his own whip. And that made only one reason for his ill-will toward Od. "Too bad Thornton didn't hang!"

Tolliver shrugged. "They say he stands in too well with the judge for that. I guess they're right. Even the Jims walk soft around him now."

He puffed reflectively at his pipe. "Thornton's changed. You wouldn't know him, hardly. Drinking hard, and the Avalon's a madhouse. Three brawls, last night I was there, and he was in all three. Well, some night there'll be another shoot-out and he'll get his. Rate he's going, I don't give him long. Wha'd you say, Miz Rothe?"

"I didn't speak. Something in my throat. Excuse me."

After Tolliver left, Berry finished up in the kitchen. She called quietly to Fabe, "Was that wise? You can't run a toll road like that — giving special rates, letting one freighter use it and refusing another. It's bound to make trouble for us. That hundred dollars is nothing but a bribe."

"I wouldn't have had to take it," Fabe retorted, "if we had the thousand you sent to Thornton!"

It was not the first time he had fretted aloud over that.

Berry winced and said no more. But by Fabe's irritation she knew he was worried again. He had realized too late that he was storing up trouble for the future. For a hundred dollars he was lined up with Tolliver against the Jims.

Berry lay staring up at the dark roof while Fabe slept heavily. She had a trick, when restless, of imagining her mind as a slate or blackboard; as an unwanted thought came she wiped it off, fighting to keep the blackboard clean.

Tonight the trick refused to work. Pictures crowded across the blackboard, fears slithering in between. She saw herself aging in this hideously lonesome place, and the next instant she saw armed men demanding to take their wagons through. Once, Od appeared, tall and smiling, well groomed, only to become suddenly a sodden and degraded wreck stumbling away.

There was a fear, among others, of never dancing again — never seeing lights and color, hearing music and laughter, or wearing pretty dresses.

Fabe had no feeling for such frivolities, no patience with any need for them. He mistrusted any impish spurt of light-heartedness. Requiring a solidly logical reason for every action, remark, laugh, he worked from dawn to dark, spoke little, and laughed not at all.

And there was the fear that what she had so readily accepted in Fabe as a boyish quality, unspoiled, might be something quite different — a stony, bumbling nature without any feeling.

She strenuously denied that fear. It was the worry and poverty and fearfully hard work that made him so taciturn. Much still remained to be done on the cabin and the road. He would not take off a minute. It was no wonder he was too weary even to express passion.

Come winter, perhaps they could take a trip to Denver. But the pass would be snowbound, part of the winter, at this altitude.

She slid out of bed and felt for her slippers. Fresh air would help. The cabin seemed oppressively close.

She crept out, wearing only her nightgown and slippers, and stretched her arms, enjoying the cool night air on her body. In the full moonlight the high crags cast jagged great shadows into the pass. She walked slowly without purpose, murmuring to herself, intent upon exorcising the hobgoblins and the knot of fear in her stomach.

"Who am I? I'm Berry Ripner — I mean Berry Rothe — and I'm young and healthy, and hopeful." She didn't feel very hopeful, but it helped a little to say so.

Fabe had bought an old spring wagon and a pair of tough little Spanish mules, cheap. The mules watched Berry drift by, and one of them took the notion to shy off and they both ran around the pen. Startled, Berry hastened away farther up the pass.

In the moonlight, pausing on a smooth patch of rock floor, she glanced down at her shadow and was reminded of a scene in a Meyerbeer opera. In that scene, she remembered, a girl lost in the bleak mountains danced with her shadow under a clear moon, to forget her loneliness.

She thought about it, recapturing it. She tentatively spun on one toe, but the nightgown wrapped itself around her knees.

On impulse she slipped the nightgown off and tossed it aside, struck a pose, spun swiftly, and danced. A song went with it, a coloratura aria; not remembering the words, she hummed it and imagined the orchestra. She felt wonderfully free and light, and without fear.

The fantastic contortions of her shadow partner amused her. She exaggerated them deliberately with her slim young body, and had to stop humming to laugh. As she did so she saw the figure of a man silently watching her.

Fabe stepped forward, demanding, "What are you doing out here this time of night? What do you think you're doing?"

"The 'Shadow Song'," she told him, with puckish gravity. "From *Dinorah*."

His face showed that he saw no humor whatever in it, nor anything else except the insane urge of a wanton. "Jumping around naked!" he snorted.

"The mules couldn't spy me here. And — and you're my husband, Fabe."

"Put something on!" he said stiffly. "This is the silliest thing I ever heard of! I think you must be crazy!"

Her shoulders slumped. She picked up her nightgown and pulled it carelessly around herself like a cloak, and walked past him back to the toll station.

He followed her in and went straight to bed.

"I didn't think you heard me go out," she said.

"I didn't. Something disturbed the mules and woke me."

"Oh, yes. The mules." She almost added, "The mules cost you a few dollars, so you heard them!"

In a little while she said, "We'll need supplies, if I'm to cook meals for Tolliver's men. And I need my clothes."

"I bought you some clothes in Quemado, didn't I?"

116

"Yes. But two house dresses and — I can't go along forever without my things. I've got to get my trunk some day, you know."

"Well, I can't spare the time," he grumbled, "and there's nobody to send. I guess you'll have to go in."

"You mean in the spring wagon? Alone?"

He was still annoyed, and he rolled over impatiently in the bed. "Why not? Women I was raised with, they thought nothing of it. I'll help you get started first thing in the morning and give you some money."

"But it'll take almost a day to get there, those mules are so slow!"

"No, you can reach Trailtown long before dark, in time to do your shopping and get your trunk. Put up at the hotel and start back next morning. Nothing to it."

She nearly laughed. Dancing naked in the moonlight, with nobody to see her — that was madness. Taking a two-day journey alone to Trailtown and back, driving a mule wagon over roads she didn't know — that was nothing.

"You're strange, Fabe," she said.

"*Me* strange!" he grunted, turning over to sleep. "*Me!*"

Having seen the night through, and counted the take and settled out the housemen's accounts, Od didn't get to bed until hours after sun-up. The town was crowded these days, trail outfits constantly arriving and departing. He had hired bartenders and floormen to help George, and four gamblers worked for the house.

He rose somewhat later than mid-afternoon, and George served him his coffee and whisky when he showed up in the barroom. Gloria looked in and saw Od, and joined him at his table.

"Don't you ever sleep any more?" Od asked her. "You were still up when I turned in."

"Sleep doesn't interest me," she yawned, bending her arms back so that her breasts thrust high, and half closing her eyes at him. "I stayed up to keep an eye on you!"

It struck Od that she spent too much time keeping her eye on him, and not enough time keeping her many men friends in line. The cause of half the fights could be traced to Gloria. But she did draw the customers in.

He finished his bracer, and to get away from her he said he had to see Ted Sieker about his riding horse that he kept at the livery.

Gloria commented sulkily that his horse took a lot of his attention, and Od replied, "Sure, a man never knows when he might want to ride."

Maybe, he thought, that was what he should do. Sell out and go off somewhere and start over. California, perhaps. He was sick of Trailtown. He was getting edgy, too, seeing Bowers around so often, his black eyes watchful, waiting for a real explosion at the Avalon. That big, crinkled face would catch him in the wrong mood one of these times, if he didn't take care, and there would be a blow-up. He'd need the fast horse then for sure.

Crossing the street, Od heard the commotion of another trail crew roaring into town after bedding their herd down along the river. Every trail crew felt impelled to put on the same show, yelling and shooting their guns off at the sky. No real harm in it, just raw exuberance. Horses danced at the hitching racks along the street, and men ran out, laughing, to hold them.

One of the foremost riders threw up a restraining hand and pointed forward. Od glanced around and saw the reason. A sunbonneted woman was driving a lop-sided old mule wagon in from the west end.

The riders stopped shooting and reined their wild-eyed ponies down, to keep from spooking the woman's mules. That was proper and usual. They were hairy and dirty from the trail, and full of mustard, but they never lost their careful consideration of womenfolks.

Od walked through the livery barn, nodding to young Ted Sieker. His horse, a tall red roan, had the best of care. It nosed Od, and he talked to it, finding a kind of peace here that eluded him elsewhere. Yes, he must set off on a long ride soon. Get away from the hard drinking that did no good, get away from everything he knew. On the outside he was prospering. Inside, he was careening downhill, going to pieces.

He came out and found Ted Sieker talking to the woman on the mule wagon, promising to water and feed the team. "Yes, sure, I'll put your rig up for the night. Glad to, ma'am."

Passing the mules, Od raised an idle glance to the face under the sunbonnet. He halted with a violent jerk of his whole body, and stood stock still. For a full minute he and she gazed silently at each other.

119

"Berry!" he said softly. "Why, Berry!" His right hand began a gesture to encompass the old wagon, the scrawny little mules, her plain, cheap dress.

He checked the gesture quickly, but too late for her not to notice. It expressed his utter shock and dismay at the change in her. The small face under the dusty sunbonnet was that of a tired woman dulled by dreary living.

He looked away, and tried to affect a poker face.

When he looked at her again she'd had time to drive the shame from her eyes. "It's nice to see you again, Berry," he made himself say evenly, whipping off his hat and stretching his hand up to her.

She took his hand, after a slight hesitation. Her hand was not the soft-skinned hand that he remembered. It felt rough. No gloves. He helped her down from the wagon as if it were a carriage.

"Thank you."

Even her voice had changed.

"You came in with your husband?"

"No, he couldn't spare the time. He's terribly busy, and works so hard —"

"Oh, yes." Od nodded and looked away again. That fool, that plodding lout, that clod! Thought more of his damned toll road than he did of his wife. "You'll be staying over the night?"

"At the hotel." She raised her head in the way he knew. "Could I get my trunk, please, if — if you still have it? I haven't been able to send for it all this time."

"Of course. It hasn't been touched. Your room is just as you left it." Holding to a neutral tone, he said, "You could use that room tonight. The hotel's packed full."

120

"I — don't believe —"

"There's a lock on the door, if you remember."

He saw her smile faintly at that, and he fingered a key from his vest pocket. "I guarantee you won't be bothered. This is the only key."

She took a breath, and bent her head, gazing down at her poor dress and her roughened hands. "*I* don't think anybody would bother me, either."

He hid the pity and rage in his eyes. "Now, how about dinner? I've got a corner table at the Chinaman's. Did you eat since this morning?"

"No, I forgot. But I have to buy some things — and really, I'm not hungry —"

"You're too tired to do shopping after that drive, and it's getting late. Let me have your list. I'll have somebody get it filled and stow the stuff in your wagon."

He took the written list and thin roll of bills that she rather helplessly gave him. "Let me walk you around to your room."

On the steps to the gallery behind the Avalon, Od stopped. "Here's your key. George will wake you up in a couple hours, with coffee. You rest till then. I'll be here at eight."

In the barroom Od said to George, "Berry is back there in her room for tonight. In two hours you take her coffee and a little brandy. And have a hot bath ready."

George elevated his brows. "Well! Like the first time she came here. Is she as bad off?"

"No," Od said. "A damned sight worse!"

He beckoned to one of the floormen. "Take this list to Bateman, and tell him to go heavy on the measures and light on the charges. I'll see him later."

He went back to the livery and gave Ted Sieker five dollars. "No charge for putting up the lady's rig, Ted, eh?"

"That's right, Od."

Then Od headed for the Chinaman's.

Berry could not restrain a tiny gasp of pure pleasure when Od guided her to the corner table a little after eight o'clock. It seemed an age since she had seen anything like this.

Two painted screens gave the table privacy; the Chinaman's wife had lent them from the living quarters for the occasion. There were tall white candles, sparkling glasses and silver, crisp white linen, and the Chinaman had donated a profusion of flowers from his garden behind the restaurant.

Od took Berry's cloak and handed it to the Chinaman's son. The boy was the same one who banged trays behind the counter every day, but tonight he was in immaculate white, silently attentive.

Od drew out Berry's chair and seated her, while his glance swept around to see that all was perfect and as he had ordered.

Berry wore emerald-green silk, a stage gown, but the best she had in her trunk. She had feared it was too extreme, but one look at the table and she knew it was right. She wore her one pair of gloves and kept them on to hide her work-roughened hands.

Od moved some of the flowers so that he could see her better, and gazed across the table at her, smiling. Her violet-blue eyes now were coming alive; they were shadowed, still tired, their slight slant inward a bit more pronounced than should be, but they were alive and young again. She had fixed her reddish-brown hair, piled it high, as she had worn it when he first met her, at the muddy Eureka Street crossing in Central City.

The Chinese boy poured cool champagne into long-stemmed glasses, the bottle wrapped meticulously in a napkin. His father entered noiselessly with a red-lacquered tray of hors d'oeuvres.

A Mexican came lounging in from behind the painted screens, elegant in full *charro* garb and carrying a huge guitar. He played softly, singing under his breath, and stationed himself in a dim corner, evidently there to stay.

"Oh!" Berry murmured, and there were tears in her eyes.

She met Od's smile, and smiled back. He had remembered the Mexican she would have danced with, and her love of music, everything. He had left out nothing.

He didn't trust himself to speak, afraid of saying the wrong thing and breaking the spell. At his slight signal the boy refilled the champagne glasses. The muted guitar and hushed voice throbbed a heartbroken song from Old Mexico.

Berry listened, her face lighting up more and more. "I never guessed you did this — I mean all this — here in Trailtown."

The Mexican's teeth flashed whitely in the dim corner, and Od said, "It's not done all the time."

"What can I say to thank you? I needed this."

"You thank me by being here. You are very beautiful."

"Thank you for that, Od, very much. You didn't think that about the woman on the wagon, I'm afraid."

"No," he frankly admitted. "But she was Berry. That was what mattered."

She studied him, wondering. His face was harder, yet it lacked some of the old assurance, and all the careless ease was gone. The edge of ready laughter had blunted. Dissipation, perhaps — he showed signs of it. Or a widening of the flaw in his character that she had felt from the first was there.

He was kind and gentle, instinctively considerate — for the present. She had known him in much this same generous mood before. She gave him credit for sincerity, while at the same time questioning its depth, seeing it as gold-leaf laid over base metal. Under the acid solvent of passion, of sharp self-interest, the base metal cropped through. The kindly man became the ruthless sharpster, the killer, the tiger.

He was unstable, victim of his own double nature. He could not be trusted. Berry sighed, and smiled at him across the table. At least his gold-leaf veneer was genuine gold; you couldn't say that about everyone, man or woman.

Food began arriving. The Chinaman could cook superbly when convinced it would be appreciated, and for this dinner he had raided his private stock and strained every effort.

The champagne, with wine at each course, relaxed Berry and loosened her tongue a little. Everything she tasted brought from her a delighted murmur that it was wonderful, marvelous.

The Chinaman and his wife and son bobbed their heads, grinning, and Od sent a bottle of wine to the Mexican, who then sang a love song that for once had a happy ending.

Berry spoke of Soft Duval. "It was Soft who helped me leave, that night. He promised to ship my trunk on to Quemado. When it didn't arrive there, I knew something must have happened to him."

Od didn't care to ask her how long she had waited in Quemado, broke and stranded, before marrying Fabe Rothe. He could hardly imagine Rothe in the role of an impatient lover pushing a whirlwind courtship. On the other hand, he could not believe that the marriage had been simply an act of desperation on Berry's part. There must have been a strong attraction. Probably both — desperation and attraction. Berry guiding, Rothe following. And Rothe certainly did have the appearance of a decent man, far above common vices.

All Od said was, "So that's what Soft was up to that night, out in front of the Avalon. I guess he loved you."

But his mind stayed on Rothe. Some of the Trailtown girls, attracted by Rothe's looks and size, had tried to work on him, one time and another. They got nowhere. They said it was like playing up to a wooden image. Od wondered about Berry, knowing that she was human, feminine, warm, not wooden.

Berry said, "I only know Soft was my good friend."

Soft Duval might have been a good friend, Od mused, but his actions that wild night had netted nothing good for Berry or anybody else. Trying to play the hand of providence, with some self-interest at heart, the old gambler had balled up the deal all around.

Dinner over, they walked slowly along the street, the night noises of the town blaring around them.

Od still had his easy stride, Berry noticed. Haste and flurry were foreign to his nature. He did everything with certainty, or at least the appearance of certainty. That, she supposed, was part of the surface. But he could also be swift and sudden.

Passing a lighted window, she caught an expression on Od's face that made her heart jump. It gave her a bad minute or two, walking in the darkness beside him around to the rear of the Avalon.

However, he halted as before on the gallery steps, hat in hand, and she thought she must have been mistaken.

"Thank you again, Od. It was wonderful."

He would keep it so. He would risk no false moves. "What time in the morning?"

"As soon as it's light. I'll say good-bye now."

"Good night, Berry. Sleep well."

Wearing her sunbonnet and house dress, and followed by two bartenders bearing her trunk, Berry entered the livery barn and was surprised to come upon the mules already harnessed up to the wagon.

126

The bartenders loaded the trunk into the wagon, nodded to her thanks, and left. Ted Sieker said to her, "Bateman sent your order over, ma'am, and here's your change."

"So much? Oh, no, he's made a mistake!"

"I doubt it. Prices have dropped."

Berry asked Ted how much she owed him, and Ted shook his head. "I never charge for little favors." He had gone all over the wagon, tightening it up so it wouldn't break down with her, and then patched the worn-out harness.

A further surprise was Od. He walked through from the back, leading a splendid red horse, saddled. "Thought I might ride out a little way with you," he remarked, tying the horse behind the wagon. "Mind?"

"I'd like it," she confessed. "Driving through town yesterday, I was nearly scared to death."

"I'll drive, then." He handed her up onto the wagon, took his seat beside her, and picked up the rope lines. "Everything stowed aboard, Ted?"

"Everything, Od."

They rode north up the street, the red horse following behind, and drew out and away from town. Berry kicked an object under the seat and bent down to see what it might be. "What's this basket?" she asked.

"Oh, the Chinaman put you up a lunch," Od replied lightly. "Some odds and ends he had left, I guess."

She rested back in the seat, sending him sidelong glances, thinking of many things. "It was nice of you to get up early on my account, Od."

He turned a grin to her. "I haven't been to bed yet."

She laughed. "I take that back, then."

To make her laugh again he began relating some of the funnier incidents that happened in the Avalon, embellishing as he went along. He could have kept it up all day, listening to her laughter and watching her face. It was over an hour before he pulled the mules to halt.

"I forgot to ask you how the toll road is coming along."

Her eyes clouded. Then she said brightly, "It's practically finished, and Fabe already has a contract. Tolliver is starting up a new freight line from the railroad to Quemado. He's contracted to use our road."

"The Jims won't like that competition," observed Od. "They're hauling to Quemado, too. There'll be trouble. Dirty trouble. No need for you and Rothe to get caught in it, though."

"No need at all."

"I suppose Rothe's putting in a grub shack? He'll want a cook for that."

"There'll be somebody."

Od stared off at a dust-devil dancing over the flats toward the first rise of low hills westward. Heat waves had already started up, making the hills quiver as though seen through flowing water. It would be another hot day.

He knew who the cook would be. Berry. Cooking for mule-skinners.

At first quietly, he asked her, "Must you go back?" And because she didn't reply, he lost control and snarled, "Go back — to *that?* You? You can't!" He pulled her to him. "Come with me. If he follows I'll kill him."

She tore loose and jumped from the wagon, falling to her knees. Her head turned. She crouched, staring up at him, and he saw the fear.

He shut his eyes for a moment, then stepped down off his side of the wagon and walked back and untied his horse. "Sorry," he said, foot in stirrup. He watched her rise up from her knees and climb to the wagon seat and gather up the dropped lines. "I'm sorry," he called after her.

She said drearily, "I'm sorry, too. But perhaps it's as well it happened. Good-bye."

Long after the mule wagon dragged through the heat waves and vanished over the low hills, he still gazed in that direction. He grew aware of sweat pouring down his face, and he mounted the red horse and rode slowly back to Trailtown.

CHAPTER
SEVEN

Heze Johns threaded through the evening crowd to Od's table in the Avalon, and jiggled an empty chair to get attention. Od was drinking, and Gloria, sitting with him, asked Heze what he wanted.

"I got news for Od," Heze said. "It's important!" He was bursting with it. He leaned close to Od, lowering his voice. "The Jims want to see you!"

"Want to see me how? With my throat cut?" Od motioned at the bottle. "Take a drink and go away!"

He was not in a humor to be patient with Heze Johns. Small things these days irritated him and made him flare up. And he knew the cause. Drinking eventually defeated its own purpose. It began by deadening the senses, and ended by corroding the nerves and laying them raw. Men were steering clear of him, distrusting his quick temper.

"Listen to me!" Heze pleaded, not realizing his recklessness. "The Jims want to talk peace with you. They're ready to meet you more'n halfway, Od."

"You've been wrong about the Jims before," Od reminded him. "Beat it!"

"But this is straight! They figure you've got a strong pull with Judge Parker. Ev'body does, o' course, since

130

he dropped that shooting charge. Ted Sieker gave it a boost, claiming he saw a wad o' cash the judge sent you! I dunno where the kid got that notion, do you?"

Od scowled at the bottle. "Nobody's fool enough to swallow that story!"

"No?" Heze snuffled a chuckle. "I've helped it along, too, ev'y chance! I figure it's to my good, well as yours, to have 'em all think you got the big law behind you."

"It's behind me, all right," Od said. He glanced over the barroom. Ray Bowers had got the habit of showing up about this time. "Right behind me, watching every step I take! He'd have exploded that myth about me and Parker long ago and let the Jims or anybody else pick my bones. But this way I'm his private business. The higher I ride now, the harder I'll fall, he figures, when he finally makes his move."

"That'll all change," Heze asserted confidently. "You'll be the kingpin again, running this town right. You're on the way. I'll be up there alonga you — maybe mayor, with your backing, like I said once before. You're the man I tie to, Od, like always. Nobody else," he confessed with pathetic frankness, "ever seems to think much o' me, I dunno why!"

"You want prestige, eh?"

Heze shook his head. "I don't care about that none," he said, without exactly knowing what it was. "I just don't want to be a gun marshal the rest o' my life. I aim to be looked up to."

His somewhat vacant eyes gazed off at visions for a moment, and came back. "Anyhow," he said, "when Jim Bloud asked me, I told him, like I do ev'body, sure you stand in good with Judge Parker. I was there, I said, at Tascosa, and I saw for myself. So Jim Bloud wants to see you. He's outside now."

Od raised his head. "You mean he'll come to me here? Well, that's something."

"Didn't I say they're ready to meet you more'n halfway?"

"Don't let Jim Bloud in here!" Gloria snapped. "He's up to some —"

"Tell him to come in, Heze," Od interrupted her. "Gloria, you better run along and play with the boys."

Behind the bar, George reached for his hip pocket the instant he spotted Jim Bloud, and let out a whistle of warning.

All the housemen quit work and stood ready. The crowd caught onto the signs, and noise died down like the last rumblings of a landslide.

Jim Bloud, holding his rolling swagger in check and looking at nobody, marched to Od's table. Od rose to meet him.

For a few seconds neither man spoke. Then Bloud growled almost shyly, "Hello, Thornton."

"Hello, Bloud. Have a seat. Drink?"

They sat down without shaking hands, Heze Johns hovering near and gesturing importantly to George and the rest to go on about their business. Heze obviously regarded himself now as a master-minding arbitrator who, having brought about a meeting of feuding chieftains, felt responsible for the success of negotiations.

132

Bloud took a drink with Od, and said, "Well, I'll come out with it. Kerry and me don't want no more trouble with you. I think it can be patched up. I think we can offer you —"

His thick-lidded eyes, sliding left and right, leveled at rest on somebody. Od followed his look and saw that Ray Bowers had come in. As had become his custom, the U.S. marshal took up position with his back to a wall; he would remain a few minutes and leave.

Od said, "It's all right. He drops in every once in a while to see how I'm doing."

"You're doing well. Damned well!" Jim Bloud stroked his heavy mustache thoughtfully. "You've sure won the trade back, since we let go our main attractions. The Silver Palace is dead. We had to tame it down. You know why. Goddam Parker, we got word he was set to —"

Od raised his glass. "Here's to absent friends. May we never hear them cursed."

"What? Oh, sure — beg pardon!" Bloud politely tipped his drink. "Look, can we talk in private? Kerry's got to be in on it, so how 'bout our office over at the freight station? You bring along anybody you want."

"Thank you. I don't need anybody." Od stumbled a little getting out of his chair. He wished he had drunk less whisky today. But after an instant's effort of will he felt all right.

Everybody in the Avalon, even the gamblers, watched them walk out together. George somberly shook his head, and Gloria almost let a playfully drunk cattleman lift her gold tiara.

Passing by Ray Bowers, Od greeted him with a bland, "Good evening, Ray!" — and in return he got a grave nod from the lawman.

In the office of the freight station Od sat facing the two Jims, bottle and glasses on the flat desk between them. He half listened to Jim Bloud's talk, while his thoughts followed a decrepit mule wagon through heat waves to the hills and on to the mountains.

Jim Bloud was telling his partner that Od even had the mighty Bowers eating out of his hand. "I saw it! That cinches it, far's I'm concerned. You, Jim?"

He drew no audible or visible response from the silent Jim Kerry, but he nodded as if he had, and turned to Od. "Thornton," he asked, "how tight is your tie-in with Parker? We've got to know. I'll tell you why in a minute."

Od drew his thoughts back from the mule wagon. "How tight do you think?" He glanced at Jim Kerry. He met Jim Kerry's expressionless, slatey stare, and it angered him. "Who says I've got any tie-in with Parker?"

"Everybody!" Jim Bloud said, laughing. "Man, you're as close-mouthed in your own way as Jim, here! But the thing's too plain. I coulda lost my shirt you'd hang for gunning Tom Brien. There, I didn't go for to bring that up. I talk too much. Now I'll tell you why we had to know."

"I don't recall I answered your question."

134

"We're satisfied." Bloud flapped a hand in dismissal of the point. "We're satisfied better'n if you bragged. Eh, Jim?"

Jim Kerry said nothing. Bloud brought his hand down flat on the desk. "All right, let's out with it. Thornton, we're gonna have trouble with Tolliver. We bought his freight business. We've poured money into it. New wagons, teams, equipment, a big payroll. It's cost a fortune. And now Tolliver's started a new freight line, to cut into us!"

"And," Od murmured, "he'll use the short-cut over the mountains to Quemado."

Both partners eyed him sharply. "You know that?" Bloud queried. He turned his head to Kerry. "We could use it, too. Yeah. It'd mean givin' up the way-stations we've built on the reg'lar road. I'd sooner not. You sure, Thornton?"

"I thought you knew."

"Didn't believe it. Didn't think that Dutchman, or whatever he is, would ever get his toll road through. Just shows how a damn fool sometimes will do a thing that a smart man won't start. Dumb luck!"

"He's lucky, all right, if he knew it."

Bloud kept slapping his palm softly on the desk, watching Od refill his glass. "Is Tolliver any partic'lar friend o' yours?" he asked.

"No," Od said. "I owe him nothing." Tolliver had always overcharged him to the limit on Avalon freight, taking sharp advantage of easygoing bookkeeping. "And for personal reasons I hate the idea of his stinking mule-skinners using that toll road!"

He didn't add that if Tolliver's wagons didn't use the toll road, Rothe would be ruined and Berry might, she just might, come back to him. He hated working with the Jims, but they could be of use to him. It was a dangerous gamble, he realized. Well, he was a gambler, wasn't he?

Bloud banged his hand down. "*Bueno! Bueno* to hell!" That phrase told more about him than a thousand words. It was a favorite among renegade raiders, smugglers, filibustering outlaws, wet cattle operators, and horse-thieves of the Rio Grande.

"We see eye to eye on that, Thornton!" he said. "Damn the toll road! Now, how 'bout Judge Parker? How rough can we get with Tolliver, without Parker sending in a pack o' marshals at us? We ain't in his good books. Not like you. That's why we want you in with us." He stopped and frowned. "What you laughing 'bout?"

Od shook his head. "Something struck me funny."

Bloud dipped a glance at the emptying bottle on the desk. "Yeah. You and us, after all our bad feeling, here we sit — I guess it's funny." He gusted a laugh, forced and false. "Funny! Just goes to show, eh? A little talk, and here we are, sitting together, having a friendly drink. It's a lesson I won't ever forget. Will you throw in with us?"

"How d'you mean?" Od refilled his glass again.

"I mean we're offering you a partnership in our freighting and trading business!" Jim Bloud said simply. "We'll sign papers to it, naming you head partner. Costs you nothing in cash, and worth plenty. All we want for it is your pull with Parker. We got to have a free hand to keep Tolliver out and block Rothe's short-cut. Quemado is coming big. There's a million dollars to be made out o' Quemado, if we tie up the freight route and play it right!"

Od laughed again, getting to his feet. "Gentlemen, your purpose is worthy, at least in regard to blocking off the toll road. Yes, indeed. You may count me in!"

He had a little trouble locating the door of the Jims' office, but found it after a search and managed to walk out without staggering. "G'night, partners!"

It seemed to him that his mind possessed an extraordinary clarity and cleverness. In the street he laughed at the Jims. Yet he was foggily aware of something wrong; he tried to locate it, couldn't just now, so he went back to the Avalon and started on another bottle.

Knowing that he shouldn't drink any more, and knowing that George knew it, he said to George positively, "I'm going to taper off and quit. I know when I've had enough."

In the freight office Bloud sighed deeply like a satisfied Indian and reached for the bottle on the desk. "Well, Jim, we put it over!" he muttered, and Jim Kerry actually cracked a smile. "That feller's headed to hell on a downhill drag!"

Od's tapering off finished the bottle. He never knew how he got to bed. Around four in the morning he awakened to the familiar dead load of uneasy guilt and self-disgust. He cursed himself and got up, vowing that he would drink no more.

"Double," he told George in the barroom, which was still crowded with roistering trail-hands. "No coffee."

George switched a small glass for a bigger one, and paused. "Double, you said, Od?"

"Yeah. I'm tapering off." Od stared at the bottle in George's hand, sincerely censuring it as a vice of which he freed himself henceforth. "One more after this and that's all."

"Sure," said George sadly. "Sure, Od. One more."

At two in the afternoon Bootjack Reid, an ex-cowhand who worked for the Jims and had stepped into Tom Brien's boots as straw boss, asked George at the bar if Od was around.

George shook his head sleepily. He allowed that Od generally roused up about this time, but no sign of him so far. To nobody would he admit that Od had staggered to bed soused.

"I'll go see if he's awake yet," Bootjack Reid said, moving off.

George started to blare, "The hell you will!" — but shut his mouth and took his hand reluctantly from his hip. He couldn't get used to the idea that Od was partners with the Jims.

He let Bootjack go, frowning after him. Maybe Od knew what he was doing; he was sharp. On the other hand, Od wasn't the same man these days, drinking hard, falling into those black moods and suddenly blowing off wild. George shook his head worriedly.

Od was dressing when Bootjack Reid knocked. He let Bootjack in and nodded toward the cigar box. "Have a smoke. What's on your mind?"

Bootjack helped himself. "Tolliver camps tonight at Little Red Spring with eight wagons for Quemado." He straddled a chair and draped his long withe of a frame over its back, adding pleasantly, "We're gonna hit him there. Jim Bloud wants you to know."

Od belted on his gun and brushed his coat, thinking about it, wishing he had been cold sober when the Jims talked peace. "Bloud in the office now?"

"In the yard. They're loadin'."

"I'll be there directly, tell him."

"Uh-huh." Bootjack Reid untangled his feet from the chair rungs and sauntered out, softly whistling a hymn that he'd picked up while night-herding somewhere.

Od came on Jim Bloud at the loading platform, cursing a roustabout for some sloppy loading. The yard was a scene of roaring confusion, out of which order somehow managed to emerge. Each huge wagon got loaded, got a final inspection, and was sent lumbering out to join the others lined up along the street. Besides freighting, the Jims were going heavily into trading on their own account. They were in business up to their necks.

"Gahdam boneheads think they know it all!" Jim Bloud growled. "Hello, Thornton. Let's go in the office. Jim's at the Palace. He don't like the noise here."

They went into the office, Bootjack following, and Od said, "What's this about Tolliver? How d'you know where he'll camp tonight?"

139

Bootjack grinned leanly, and Bloud answered, "We got a man in his crew! We know ev'ry move Tolliver makes. We let him send a wagon over Rothe's road, for pilot. Damn wagon got through to Quemado and cut the time down by nearly three full days! That means Tolliver could shave his freight rates below ours and beat us out. Now he's heading there with eight wagons, loaded high. We'll stop 'em! Bootjack's got a kinda idea."

"What is it?"

"*Bandidos*," murmured Bootjack, shrugging modestly. "We sing out in Mex'can an' jump the camp in the dark. Afterward, for the looks of it, we burn the wagons."

"It won't do," Od said. He matched his tone to Bootjack's; they could have been discussing the merits of tar and tallow as axle grease. "We've never had a Mexican raid this far from the border since I can remember. Judge Parker, Bowers — any lawman who knows the score would know where to look."

"Sure," Bloud acknowledged. "We know. It's only meant to provide 'em a false trail, a blind. It falls on you to see they oblige us by taking it."

"Who do you think I am?"

"Head partner o' this firm, as is now well known. The law will talk to you first. You're our cover."

"What you've got in mind," Od said, "nobody could ever cover. No, it won't do. Too rough! Raid Tolliver's camp, yes. Stampede his mules and run 'em clear off. Leave him and his crew afoot and his wagons stranded. That'll stop him."

140

"For how long?"

"Who knows? Repeat the treatment till he gets discouraged and calls it quits. But no killing, robbery, burning, or we'll all be seeing Judge Parker!"

Bloud tugged at his black mustache, staring discontentedly out into the wagon yard. "I thought you and him —"

"There's a limit," Od dryly interrupted, "to what even I can do. The judge has sworn to put down lawlessness in this district. I wouldn't want to strain his patience *too* far."

Bloud's heavy face came around with a hard and stubborn look on it. "That's the way we'll do it, then. You hear, Bootjack?"

"Just a harmless little caper, huh?" Bootjack Reid fluttered long fingers in mock delicacy. "An' we don't gun nobody — not even Tolliver if he climbs in the sights!"

"I'll ride along with you tonight," Od said, and the two looked at each other and shrugged.

The Jims' horsemen sat waiting in the darkness, eyes fastened on the distant speck of light that marked Tolliver's camp at Little Red Spring.

Tolliver as yet maintained no regular road stations along his route, simply making use of the handiest camp sites. On that count he still was a wildcat freighter, although it was said that he could now put thirty wagons into service. He kept his overhead expenses low and could underbid and get all the hauling business he could handle.

The waiting horsemen numbered nine, all told. Od did not recognize any of them as roustabouts from the Jims' wagon yard. Mostly they were of Bootjack Reid's type: ex-cowhands who had come a cropper through one thing or another, and had gravitated naturally to a deadfall dive such as the Silver Palace. They looked as if they had been around, and done things that they wouldn't willingly talk about. All were well armed with Colts and Winchesters.

Bootjack Reid tramped back from scouting the Tolliver camp and said, "All sleepin'. No guard."

He sank down and squatted on his high heels, pointing carefully, cupping his voice with his hand. "The mules are on the left, a bit back. A rope corral. We don't need to cut it, or I would've. The mules'll bust it."

He twisted his head to look up at Od. "It suit you?"

At Od's side Jim Bloud called softly, "It suits fine!" A wild note rang through his muted voice. "Pull your guns, boys, we're going in!"

Od heeled the red horse forward a jump and reined it around broadside to the group. "This is only a scare raid, remember! We don't shoot to kill anybody!" He turned angrily on Bloud. "Dammit, this isn't the border country. All we're here to do is stampede some mules."

His angry outburst clearly surprised the riders. They knew of his reputation, and evidently they had not been warned of any limits to this raid. He was the last man they would have expected to call for half-measures. They could only take it as evidence of broken nerve. They knew that some of the best, the famed hot-shots,

142

suddenly folded, went chicken, ran out. The men tightened up uneasily, disliking going into action behind a has-been. Od felt it.

The eyes of the men shone in the darkness, coolly considering him, and he felt classed as an outsider in their night-riding company. They took their pay from the Jims and questioned the right of anyone else to lay out orders to them. They did not accept him as leader, regardless of the signed agreement that named him head of the firm. He was the boss on paper, but the man they served was Jim Bloud.

Bloud said, "No call to get bowed up, Thornton. We know what we're here for. Let's get on with it before you wake 'em up."

The words, with their dry hint of criticism, fetched a sardonic chuckle from Bootjack Reid, and the men lounged more loosely in their saddles, exchanging nods.

In the opinion of the men, Od judged, Bloud had put him down a notch. They approved. From here on nothing he did would be right. They were a hard-bitten breed, as stubborn in their prejudices as in their loyalties. Od passed it off, not caring enough to let it trouble him.

They put their horses on, holding them to a walk. The thin swish of hoofs in dried grass, and low thumping on sandy soil, raised a steady noise that could not be hushed. The lounging riders tensed up, approaching Tolliver's camp.

Od leaned forward like the rest, staring ahead. He raised an arm, signaling a halt. The straight-sided freight wagons bulked up plain and black against the low campfire. Shapes humped in bedrolls lay strewn around the fire like bits of baggage carelessly thrown anywhere. Od heard the mules moving restlessly in their rope corral beyond the camp.

He didn't like this raid. In his past he'd taken some long chances, and come out laughing. But there was no laughter in this. Perhaps, he thought, George was right and these riders were right. Perhaps he really had become a has-been, due for destruction.

"We skirt around on the whoop and hit the corral," he murmured. "Shoot high. We okay, Bloud?"

"*Bueno* to hell!" Bloud sang out, and that set it off.

Od heeled the red horse forward to a dead run, angling to the left to pass the camp, drawing his gun and letting loose a shot skyward. The rest followed, raising the long, screeching Texas yell. In the midst of it Bloud shouted something that Od couldn't catch.

The riders, Bloud at their head, veered out from behind Od and thundered headlong at the wagons to charge right through Tolliver's camp. Od heard them fall away from behind him, and threw a glance around and saw their move. The straight attack was too prompt to be a sudden hot impulse. Bloud and Bootjack had kept their minds on a wipe-out raid, and the riders simply fell in with the murderous purpose of this night's ride.

The bedded shapes around the fire of Tolliver's camp did not stir, in spite of the racket of running horses, yelling men, spurting guns. That fact rang a chill warning, and when rifle fire ripped from the freight

144

wagons Od was ducked low over his saddle-horn and streaking past.

He heard the fluttery scream of a hard-hit horse and the leather-snapping crash of its fall. A hurt man cursed, his voice wailing in the uproar of exploding cartridges. The mad yelling of the riders broke off, urgent dismay abruptly driving out glee.

From the shot-spearing wagons somebody — most likely Tolliver, who could take a fight when it ran his way — shouted, "Come an' git it, you Jims! We're ready and we got plenty for all!"

It was a challenge, but Bloud called out, "Pick 'em up an' let's get out o' this bust!" He sounded calm, being the kind of man who kept his head best in a bad scrape.

The mules were not only corralled, but picketed for extra precaution, something that Bootjack Reid had overlooked on his scout. Well over a hundred of them, disturbed by the sudden noise, stamped and crowded nervously together, and when Od swirled out of the darkness they spooked. Od blazed two shots over their upflung heads and sent them off in a snorting tangle.

Given some help, or a little more time, he could have stampeded the whole bunch. As it was, about half of them broke out of the corral, trailing ropes and picket stakes. He had to settle for that much, because men came running from the wagons, firing at him. The red horse whirled under rein and stretched out, racing.

Coming upon Bloud and the others a mile back, he sang out to make himself known and rode up to them.

Two of the men were riding double. Bootjack carried a body slung awkwardly across his knees, and was having some trouble with his horse, which didn't like it.

The ugly temper of the men struck Od's senses like heat, though they said nothing.

Bloud put it into words. "We got a dead man. Shorty Willis. And two hurt. Thornton, your gahdam raid was a bust!"

"My raid?" Od said. "*Mine?* Stampede the mules, I said — not shoot up the camp. They were ready for you. If you ask me, Tolliver's got a man planted in *your* crew!"

Bootjack inquired, "Meanin' anybody in partic'lar?"

"If I did, you know I'd name him."

"Somebody maybe talked in the wrong company," Bloud argued. "It coulda been you, Thornton."

"Or you, Bloud."

The thing was sliding toward a dangerous split that would benefit nobody, and Od decided to break it off. He said, "I advise you to keep tonight's affair quiet. Tolliver will, I guess. It seems to suit him to do his own fighting. Next time, keep your mind on the mules. I was able to run off about half. It'll hold Tolliver up a while, but we could've done better if you and your haywire trigger men hadn't got so damned itchy for a kill."

He touched his horse and left them.

After a minute Bloud spoke to Bootjack. "Take Shorty off somewhere an' cover him up till you can bury him. We can't lug a dead man into Trailtown like this, if Bowers is still there. Bound to be questions."

146

"Is that," Bootjack drawled, "what the big boss meant?" Shorty Willis had been his side-kick. Bootjack resented the callous dismissal of Shorty's corpse, but he inclined to lay it against Od Thornton.

Bloud shot him a glare. "Big boss, hell! I give the orders!" Then, sensing the lean ex-cowhand's mood, he said less harshly, "Lay poor Shorty away till we can bury him decent. We'll give him a real first-class funeral when we get around to it. I know how you feel."

"Sure," Bootjack said. "I know you do."

Bloud nodded. He didn't give a damn for Shorty Willis or anybody else. He said, "Bootjack, when we get back to town I want you to take a crew with fresh horses and anything else you need, and go wreck that damn toll road! Anybody tries to stop you, shoot and to hell with it, I don't care who! Clear?"

"Sure. Good as done." Bootjack patted Shorty's stiffening back. "Shorty told me he saw a funeral once, St. Louis or some place, an' the horses wore black feathers. Reckon we could do that?"

CHAPTER
EIGHT

"This'll do to start," Bootjack said, at a bridged-over gap in the toll road.

His men pulled up and dismounted. Two of them unloaded picks and crowbars from the pack horse and passed them out. They were roustabouts, picked for muscle and ability to work fast and fight dirty for a ten-dollar bonus.

Looking up along the empty toll road clinging to the canyon wall, Bootjack could see other log bridges such as this one. In the early dawn, shadow made the canyon there appear bottomless, while down here it shallowed out and the wall became a steep bank. For a wagon, though, a rolling tumble of a hundred yards was as bad as a mile drop, so this was as good a place as any to begin.

"Leave room for us to cross," he said. "We'll knock out all we can up yonder an' finish 'em off as we come down."

For this job he had men who said they could ride horse-back. They were drifters, drunkards, buffalo tramps, and men out of law, but they had one virtue which saddle-men lacked: they pitched in at a work job without figuring all day how to do it from the saddle with a rope. And for the extra pay they would take any chance.

"Not so much noise, if you can help it," said Bootjack, as pried logs bounced down the canyon.

The man he spoke to raised a sweating face and a bloodshot stare. Bootjack slipped his carbine out of its saddle scabbard.

You couldn't ever tell about these boozy cutthroats that the Jims put on their payroll for cheapness. Bash your head in with a crowbar and forget it in five minutes. They did get the work done, though, doing it in a kind of frenzy that ignored bruises and cuts. The work stood in the way to their extra pay; they smashed at it, hating it as an obstacle.

For routine caution he glanced back down the road.

His eyes widened, then slitted. Two riders, having rounded a bend of the road, had halted to watch the workers.

Bootjack brought up his carbine. He had ridden for the Bootjack cattle outfit on the Canadian, where he got his name, until he went to rustling; thereafter his impulse was to send a shot at strangers and wave them around his camp. He didn't figure to hit either of the two, until his carbine leveled and he remembered what he was here to do.

The two riders saw his movement. They slung their horses fast around and vanished. Bootjack fired too late and lowered his carbine, swearing. The report rattled echoes up and down the canyon. The crew's mounts tossed their heads.

"You oughta flagged 'em on, then dropped 'em!" one of the roustabouts criticized him. "Who was they?"

"I don't know," Bootjack said.

His private suspicion was that they were riders for Tolliver, scouting the route for possible trouble. In that case there might be others. Bootjack was bothered by the strength and assurance that Tolliver had shown in meeting last night's raid and beating it off. To account for it, Tolliver must have hired some pretty tough gun-guards.

"Finish this off," he told the men. "We won't go no further. That shot's goin' to bring somebody down from the toll station. I don't want to be caught here two ways an' no cover."

They completed the destruction of the bridge, leaving a yawning gap in the road.

It was while they loaded their tools on the pack horse that the first gunfire smashed at them from the bend down the road. The man doing the packing let it go and fell into the jangle of spilled picks and crowbars, causing the pack horse to jump clear and go barging in among the saddled mounts.

Bootjack leaped onto his horse. It danced a circle, but the thoroughly wrecked bridge barred escape up over the pass. Men down at the bend, kneeling and standing, sighted their shots. Bootjack rode at them, sitting up straight, reins loose and his carbine spitting.

The riflemen at the bend did not waver. They kept on firing.

Bootjack slung the carbine around and hit his horse on the rump, and used rein and spur, forcing it off the

150

road, over the edge, down the canyon bank. The horse hurtled down, head low, strained hind-quarters scraping, slithering from one side to the other, to the bottom.

Bootjack looked up and back. Having no other escape from the gunfire, the roustabouts, those still able, were trying to follow his example. They didn't have his horsemanship; they plunged down, hanging to mane and saddle horn, bumping wildly.

Two lost out, their horses stumbling to a sprawl, one careening a full somersault and pitching the rider ten feet in the air.

Had they been of his own kind Bootjack would have turned back for them. For these men he had no comradeship, no feeling. He saw the heads of the Tolliver men bob up above the edge of the road to stare and fire down at him and the remnant of his laboring crew.

He raised the carbine, took careful aim, fired. A head jerked and lolled over. "That's one for Shorty," Bootjack said aloud, and he rode on.

Which one didn't interest him. The fight was on, and that one belonged on the wrong side.

Od saw, from the doors of the Avalon, Bootjack Reid and the roustabouts troop into Trailtown. He had been about to go to bed, later than usual, mid-morning. After watching Bootjack climb stiffly off his tired horse and clump into the freight office, Od put off sleep and went on over. He hadn't seen Jim Bloud since last night's quarrel.

Entering the office, Od listened to the tail-end of Bootjack's report to Bloud, who nodded abstractedly to him while his heavy face flared red as Bootjack finished speaking.

The road-wrecking party was news to Od. He should have known, he guessed, that Bloud would think of that. It was the obvious thing to do next, the raid on Tolliver's camp not succeeding.

Bloud said, "All right, Bootjack. Another bust! By God, that's enough, ain't it, Jim?"

Jim Kerry, at the desk, glanced up and nodded, and Bloud went on: "We been cat-footin' where we oughta tromp! It never pays, I've found. You got to slam 'em down, put the boots to 'em, break 'em!" He slanted a speculative look at Od. "You agree?"

Od shrugged. "It depends."

Bloud turned his back on Od and spoke again to Jim Kerry. "We'll take ev'ry man we got, eh, Jim? Take the Dutchman's road, jump Tolliver —"

He felt Od's hand on his shoulder, and looked at it and then over it at Od's face. Bootjack, tired as he was, leaned his long body forward slightly, his eyes flicking from one man to the other.

"Wait a minute," Od said to Bloud. "The Dutchman thinks a lot of his road. You'd have to kill him!" He recalled the Duke's girl, how Bloud had beaten her up, broken her jaw. "He's got his wife there."

Bloud pulled his shoulder away. "I know. So does ever'body. She's *your* pers'nal little problem. You handle her — or we will. I say we've had enough cat-footin'. We take the Dutchman's road!"

152

"I don't agree," Od said, and stepped back. "I won't stand for it! Nor will Parker. Nor Bowers."

Bloud swung his thick-set body around and stared at him. At the desk, Jim Kerry raised his expressionless face from a ledger, eyes more narrowed and straighter than ever.

Bloud said, "Thornton, we took you in the firm for cover. So far, you been a brake on us. A hoodoo. I think you better loose up."

"It was you made the deal. I'm telling you what you can't do." Od shifted to put Bootjack into sight. "You can't raid the toll station. That's flat."

Their eyes bored at him. Very calmly, Bloud remarked, "You're tellin' again what we can't do. S'pose you tell us what we *can* do."

Od thought fast. In this camp he was purposely a bad-luck Jonah, deliberately the renegade for the sake of Berry. His double-play was about over. He had paid out nearly all his rope, and a kink now would snap apart the whole works.

"You can buy Rothe's road," Od said, "and close it down, or use it. He needs money, I believe."

Bloud cut a hand through the air in a violently dismissing gesture. "More money out — an' us scraping the barrel! Hell, no!" He swung aside and spoke to Jim Kerry. "Do we, Jim?"

Kerry scribbled for a minute. He slowly raised a finger.

Jim Bloud growled wrathily, "Damn! I think my way's better. But if you say so, I'll send the Dutchman an offer. By God, he better grab it, Thornton, or I swear we'll —"

"That's understood," Od said, leaving.

His thoughts gnawed on the certainty that he had reached the limit and made the last possible play. He could not stall off the Jims any longer on his precarious bluff. Bitterly dissatisfied, they were growing suspicious. It had trembled on a hair-line balance until Kerry gave the sign. He hoped Fabe Rothe would prove reasonable to the Jims' offer to buy the toll road. If Rothe got bull-headed about it, then the game was shot and hell to pay all around.

At the Avalon he came upon Ray Bowers in his customary position, his back to the wall, earlier than usual. This time Gloria stood talking with him, her golden head thrown back, bright eyes and red lips deliberately provocative. Bowers showed a curiously reluctant interest in her.

Keyed up and edgy, Od swerved over and stated abruptly, "You're taking up room on my property, Bowers. I don't run a free-lunch stand for federal officers. Buy a drink or get out!"

George hunched behind the bar, grunting loudly and touching his gun-weighted hip pocket. Those words of Od's brought a return of the good days when Od laid the tough word down on the line to everybody and anybody. The Avalon housemen on duty froze, hands to weapons, more or less ready to shoot or knife or brass-knuckle for the house.

Bowers's crinkled face didn't change, although his small round eyes sharpened. "Champagne for the lady," he murmured. "Nothing for me."

154

Od walked on to the bar, watching Bowers suddenly bend toward Gloria and whisper to her. Bowers knew what she was, but so had dozens of other men who had gone broke on her. Gloria had a trick of convincing every man that he was the real one, the only one, that the others didn't count.

Laughing, making a mouth at him, Gloria shook her head. But she didn't leave him. She swayed a little closer. Ray Bowers flushed and dug into his pocket to pay for the champagne. He brought out a thick roll of bills. Gloria laughed again, warmly.

Still watching, Od hoped Gloria would take up more and more of Ray Bowers's time.

"They slowed my time some, yes," Tolliver admitted to Fabe Rothe in the toll station.

He poured himself a drink from the bottle that he had brought in with him. "I won't make much of a profit on this haul. But they didn't stop me, Rothe! Nor they ain't going to! I'll smash 'em! Before I'm through, they'll come begging to me to buy 'em out! They don't chouse ol' Tolliver! I'm a pure cactus booger from way back, and I got bronco in my blood!"

Worriedly, Fabe Rothe ran fingers through his fair hair. "I didn't look to get in trouble. It's bad for business." He had given up shaving as a waste of time, and the curly fuzz on his face lent him an oddly bearish appearance. "No profit in fighting!"

"No profit in it for *them!*" said Tolliver. "We broke up their raid and got every mule back. We fixed the road good as new, and got the wagons over. If that's the best they can do, I've got 'em beat!"

Berry came to the kitchen door. "Will it be like this every time, Mr. Tolliver?" she asked. She had cooked for sixteen hungry men and now was cleaning up, but that wasn't what she meant. "Or won't it get worse?"

"No!" Tolliver declared, while Fabe Rothe motioned impatiently at Berry to go back into the kitchen. "I'm free to say I was a little anxious when Od Thornton threw in with the Jims. I expected real big trouble. It ain't come. Just small mischief, is all. They're holding back. I guess the truth is, they're plain scared of me!"

Berry doubted it. Fabe, however, nodded seriously and made mention of a message he had received. "Fellow that came up this morning brought it. The Jims — and Thornton — want to buy my road. It shows they'd sooner not make trouble, don't it?"

Tolliver laughed. "It sure does! Yeah, I got 'em huntin' cover, all right! Your answer is, they can't buy this road nor use it at any price! You write 'em that, hear?"

His spirits ran high. He had got his eight wagons successfully over the pass and seen them off toward Quemado. Six more were coming down from the railhead, and he was riding back to meet them and pilot them through.

"I will," Fabe Rothe promised. He tried for an ingratiating smile. "Mr. Tolliver, your men eat so good we're out of grub again. I need some money."

Tolliver drew out a fat roll and peeled off some bills. "Here you are. Say, I can ship you in your supplies if you want."

"No, thank you all the same," said Fabe, taking the money. "My wife gets real bargains in Trailtown. And she can take in my answer to the Jims, and save the post." He got a thought. "I'd reckon you'd want some of your riders along, going back."

Tolliver shook his head, smiling slyly down at his glass. "They got a job to do. I'll teach Thornton and the Jims not to mess with me!"

When he was gone, Berry said earnestly, "Fabe, you shouldn't let that man boss you. He's pulling us into his trouble. I think it's a lot worse than he realizes. He's much too confident!"

Fabe stared coldly at her. Of late his blue eyes had taken on a stony mask whenever she ventured any suggestion concerning the toll road, as if he wished her to understand that it was *his* toll road and no partnership with her was involved.

"You don't know what you're talking about!" he snapped. "And another thing — I'll ask you to keep out of it when I'm talking business with Tolliver. Folks will think I let my wife run me!"

"I'd say, dear, that you were joking, except I know you *never* joke."

He didn't answer.

Johnny Cisneros, boss gun-guard for Tolliver, climbed up over the ridge-rock and said to the four waiting

157

men, "They're coming. Let's don't shoot too quick, eh?"

He said it gently, as if asking a favor, not giving a command. The four men were Texans, and even after years as a top hand and then *segundo* on the old Bootjack outfit he still kept his awareness of the average Texan's resentment of a Mexican boss. Not that he was actually a Mexican, having been born and raised well north of the Rio Grande, but he was of the race.

Yet he knew that he need not let it worry him. He had proved his quality many times to them. With the old Bootjack outfit broken up and gone to hell, and they on the loose, taking fighting-pay from anybody who would hire them, by unspoken agreement they still elected him their leader. He was proud of that, but he held to his habit of cautious courtesy.

They stubbed out their cigarettes and lay watching the road below them. Each gave his rifle a final inspection, and set out a row of cartridges in easy reach. The road here, the Jims' wagon route, drew a long curve around the Mockingbird Hills. This made the only bad section on the route, for the road rose steeply up and over a saddleback and dropped as steeply down again.

One of the four men asked Johnny Cisneros if he thought Bootjack Reid might be with the oncoming freight wagons. Johnny replied that he didn't figure on it.

The man said, "He was the joker who stopped an' put a bullet in Bim on the toll road, no mistake. You got

158

a look at him, Johnny, an' you know it. You an' him rid for the outfit longer'n anybody. You was friends."

"Not now," said Johnny Cisneros. Bootjack Reid rode for the wrong side now. "There's the first wagon. Good mules, eh? I'd sooner kill the drivers, swear to God, but Tolliver said the mules and he's paying, what the hell."

The Jims' teamsters hitched up double-teamed to drag each huge wagon grinding up the grade. Familiar with the job, they worked in a fearful din, cursing, cracking whips, expertly angling the wagons into place on the saddleback. The last wagon lurched up, was halted, and much of the noise subsided. The teamsters swigged from bottles and lighted pipes, and got the chains ready to lock the rear wheels on the downgrade ahead.

After the breathing spell, a shout started the leading wagon and the train got ponderously into motion. As the wagons tipped forward to the downgrade, even the chained wheels could not prevent a slowly gathering momentum. Deep ruts scored in the road showed that this was usual. The mules began shuffling into a half-trot. The high wagons swayed, but the ruts held them to the road.

"I think we could shoot now, maybe, eh?" said Johnny Cisneros.

At the first crackle of rifle fire three mules of the leading wagon dropped. The team ran over them, and tangled, and the wagon hit them and crunched to a sudden standstill; it yawed over and the teamster took a surprised header off the box, but it rocked upright again.

The wagon behind it, following too close, hadn't a chance to avoid a collision. The mules shied aside, but the wagon slithered on and crashed into the first. It made a pile-up that blocked the road.

The teamster on the third wagon, unable to halt, tried to swerve around on the low side. He lined his mules out, hard over, cramping his front wheels and jumping them out of the ruts. He almost scraped past.

His off wheels sank in the sand. The wagon staggered, seemed to fight to regain its losing center of gravity, and capsized, spilling boxes and sacks of merchandise everywhere. The teamster jumped, but on the wrong side. The wagon fell on him. He screamed.

"I sure do hate to kill those good mules," said Johnny Cisneros. "Let's hit that fourth wagon now, eh? I think we can do the same for that sonna beetch."

CHAPTER
NINE

Finishing his wake-up coffee and whisky, Od paced to the front door of the Avalon and looked out indifferently at the street in the hot afternoon.

The sun struck at his eyes and he rubbed their lids gently with spread thumb and forefinger, trying to remember when and how he had got to bed. He lighted a cigar. It tasted wrong. Everything did.

Gloria glided up behind him and slid a hand over his shoulder, saying, "Off to visit your horse again, honey? Some day I'll shoot the brute."

He shifted restlessly and pushed on outside, but she kept close to him, making sinuous movements against him, murmuring in his ear. She, too, he guessed, knew something about the hunger of loneliness.

He patted her hand, soft on his shoulder, but then he saw Ray Bowers emerge from the hotel and start up the street, and his mood changed.

Bowers was around all the time now, silent and watchful. He spoke only to Gloria, in undertones, and bought champagne for her at fifteen dollars a bottle. Gloria adored champagne and had got dazzlingly high the last couple of times. Bowers drank nothing.

The lawman sighted Od and Gloria close together outside the door of the Avalon. His strange face crinkled a little deeper. He stopped to inspect the horses tied up at Bateman's hitching rack. He never lounged, never relaxed the tautness of his tall, well-built body. He simply stood there on the boardwalk, erect, arms straight down at his sides, stiff-brimmed hat square on his head, like an Indian.

Bowers certainly had some Indian blood, Od thought. His timeless patience and undying grudge pointed to it, as well as his blank look and severely grave manner like that of a fanatical monk; or a chieftain who had been misused and cheated, made a fool of, made small.

Od took his glance off Bowers and sent it ranging idly up the street. His eyes fastened instantly on a lopsided old mule wagon driven by a woman in squatter house dress and sunbonnet.

He wasn't aware that he jerked and moved forward. Gloria said harshly, "Yes, here she comes again! Did you get your money's worth the last time? Did that damn little —"

Instinctively he laid the back of his hand against her mouth. It was hardly a blow, but rather a muffling gesture to stem her off.

Furious, Gloria screamed, "You hit me, you — !" She swore at him.

And suddenly Ray Bowers stood planted squarely in Od's path.

"Marshal, this is not a law matter," Od reminded him. "This is personal."

"It is personal," Bowers agreed, "in more ways than one."

"That's clear," Od said, and crossed to the livery stable. He wondered briefly at a man like Bowers falling for Gloria. Maybe Bowers, too, knew something about loneliness.

The pair followed him with their eyes. "I'm going to break him, any way I can," Bowers stated, calmly positive. "Now is it all right with you?"

Gloria touched her lips with her fingers. People in the street regarded her curiously, some of the men grinning. They had seen the incident; there would be jokes at her expense.

"It's all right," she said. "You do that, honey."

"Good," Bowers murmured. He took her arm. His round eyes, black and hard, gentled. "Champagne?"

Od was waiting at the livery stable when Berry drew in. Hat held at his thigh, he asked her, "Can I help you? I want to."

She shook her head. She looked, to him, even more work-worn and beaten than before. She was not beautiful. But she was Berry.

"No, thank you," she said, and drew a folded paper from the pocket of her dusty, faded dress.

She had not yet unpacked her trunk; she hadn't the heart. Fabe disapproved of gay theatrical garb.

"I have a message from my husband, to the firm of Thornton, Bloud, and Kerry. Will you take it, please?"

Od took it. After he read the curt message he crammed the paper into his coat pocket. Its import did not surprise him, but it did dismay him. He kept his

163

face blank, however. "Berry, please don't go back up there. Stay here for a while, will you?"

He saw the refusal in her face. He spread his hands, letting his hat fall. "Very well. I can't help you. But will you let old George — and Heze Johns — squire you around?"

"George, yes. And Mr. Johns." She could trust those two.

Od bowed to her. He hurried back to the Avalon.

"George," he said, "drop everything and take care of Miss Berry. You and Heze. See she is not charged half, and —"

Sudden despair caught him. He stared at George, blindly.

"Don't worry," George said. "We'll take good care of her. She's a good kid. I'll never forget how she danced that night —"

"Yes," Od said. "You and Heze take care of her."

He thought for a minute. "Her husband's scared to come in. He's gone over to Tolliver. So he sends her in. If there's any trouble, I'll be there. Just give me a yell."

There was not trouble. George and Heze escorted Berry around and evidently enjoyed it, two old bachelors sporting gallant airs. They did her shopping, took her to dinner, and got her a room all to herself in the crowded hotel.

"There she goes," said George in the early morning. Young Ted Sieker was seeing Berry off from the livery stable. "She's pretty swell, that gal." Against his stern bachelor principles, George added, "Damned good kid!"

Od watched the mule wagon trundle up the street. "Yes. And such a damn' little fool!"

George frowned. "She'd do to take along," he observed.

"She would," Od said. "She sure as hell would!"

Od paid a call on Ray Bowers at the hotel.

Although the morning was still early, Bowers was up and dressed. At Od's knock he opened the door and, seeing who it was, he stepped back, right hand sliding under his coat.

Od walked in past him and sat on the unmade bed. His mission being driven by final extremity, he made himself harmless and vulnerable, placing his hands out wide on the edge of the bed.

"Look, Bowers," he said. "It's a freighter war, all right. It's going to get bad. I mean *bad!* And real soon!"

Bowers nodded, smiling. "I know."

Od got up and stepped to the window, to avoid showing the rage that came from looking at that chill, vindictive smile. He put his back to Bowers. "The Jims are in a hole. They'll get out of it by killing those who're in their way. They've got a bad bunch there on their payroll."

"I know," Bowers said. "Tolliver, too."

"Tolliver's hired a few shooters, yes. But nothing like the army of cutthroats the Jims have got. Tolliver's big ace is the toll road. He can sit tight. The Jims can't. They've got too much money tied up. Next move is theirs."

"I know. What do you hope to get from me?"

"Put on some of your deputies to guard the toll road. That's where it'll strike." Od turned from the window. "I ask you —"

"Keep asking me, Thornton. I like to hear it." Bowers still smiled. "It's got out of hand on you, eh? You want me to pull your chestnuts out of the fire. The answer is no."

Od held himself in. "You're a peace officer, aren't you? You're the United States marshal of this district, aren't you?"

Bowers's face tightened. "Didn't I tell you this is personal? Hell, man, I've been staying here in Trailtown against orders — waiting for a break. I'm way out of favor with Judge Parker. Don't ask me for deputies. I couldn't provide 'em even if I would. Officially, I'm a dead duck unless I pull a coup here. That means you. Is that straight? Now get out!"

"You told me once you never swore false witness," Od said to him. "I believed you. I took it to mean —"

"Get out!" Bowers repeated. He looked a century old. "Get out, damn you!"

Od slept until noon, and George fired up a hot bath for him at Gloria's urging.

While Od soaked in the bath, Gloria slipped into his room and delved into the right-hand pocket of his coat. She had seen Berry give him a note, seen its effect upon him, and she was fiercely curious to know what it contained.

She read it in the privacy of the ladies' rest room. It was disappointing, not at all what she had expected, but

166

she kept it. Perhaps Ray Bowers would know what to make of it.

She drifted out to the front door of the Avalon and looked for Ray; it was about time for him to show up and start buying her champagne. She tapped an impatient toe, paying no heed to a man who clattered up from the south on a bareback mule and legged off and ran into the Jims' freight office.

Ray Bowers stalked up to her fifteen minutes later, saying, "Hi, Goldie!" His pet name for her, and it sounded silly on his lips. "Little commotion over there at the freight office. I had to look into it. Champagne?"

Gloria sat with him in the Avalon and drank champagne, and after the third glass she produced the note.

Ray Bowers read it carefully, then lifted his head as Od came into the barroom from the rear.

At that moment Bootjack Reid entered by the front door. He paced directly to Od. The two spoke. Od shook his head at George, who was pouring coffee and whisky, and left with Bootjack.

"Is this note all?" Bowers muttered to Gloria. "Come clean with me, Goldie! He didn't even look at you! Or didn't you notice?"

"I noticed!" Gloria said.

She leaned forward on the table, talking in a whisper, while Bowers refilled her glass and signaled George for another bottle.

Ray Bowers's roll of bills was getting skinny, George noted professionally, when Bowers paid him the fifteen dollars. Bowers had spent a lot, the last few days. For smiles. And yet with some brashness and a hundred-dollar bill Bowers could have —

Well, it took all kinds, as the old lady said when she kissed the cow. You couldn't predict rightly what any man would do. Nobody could have figured that Ray Bowers would ever be a sucker for a dance-hall queen. At the same time, it was out of all reason for Od Thornton to be hitting the bottle so hard, going haywire. Everybody in this country took a loco turn sooner or later, George guessed, except himself. He was too burned-out for such foolishness. He'd had his day, and all that concerned him personally now was his fallen arches, which ached his feet.

The Jims' office was in an uproar. Bloud stamped up and down, cursing. Jim Kerry thumped a fist repeatedly on a ledger, saying nothing. Their gun-riders stood around, loudly talking war.

Bloud lit into Od as soon as he entered the office. "You know what they done?" he bawled. "You know what?"

"Muzzle it!" Od said. "D'you want the whole town and half of Texas to hear you?"

Bloud lowered his head like a bull buffalo. His double chin swelled out redly. In rage he looked grotesque, a gross caricature of the cool and able man that he became when in action.

He stabbed a thick forefinger at Od. "To hell with the town! Don't tell me how to talk, you hoodoo! Tolliver's riders jumped our wagon train in the Mockingbirds and shot it up! Wrecked seven wagons!"

Od exclaimed, "Well, I be damned! That's to pay us for our raid at Little Red. Tolliver must be feeling pretty big."

He thought then of the inevitable consequences. Reprisal had to crowd swiftly upon reprisal. The freighters' war had exploded wide open, as Ray Bowers had predicted it would.

"Those Tolliver jiggers will head for Quemado," Od said. "They'll join Tolliver's wagons there. They'll start back with 'em to Rothe's toll road. If we make time, we'll hit 'em somewhere along the road before they —"

"The hell we will!" Bloud broke in. "Nothin' like it!"

He eyed Od up and down. "Thornton, your ideas stink. Tolliver's piloting his second string of wagons down from the railhead. By now he should be crossing the mountains on the short-cut. Those damned gun-riders of his are way off, scooting around to Quemado after shooting up our train. Do I have to tell you what *my* idea is?"

"No, I can guess. You want a wipe-out, eh?"

"Sure — it's what I've wanted all along. That's my way. I've found you can get away with anything, if you do it big!"

"You tried it at Little Red," Od reminded him. "It was a bust."

"This time it won't be." Bloud swore. "We'll take every man we've got who can use a gun or knife! Tolliver ain't got sharpshooters with him this trip. He'll make slow time in the mountains, and camp when it's dark."

Fishing for Bloud's full intentions, Od observed, "That'll be beyond the toll station, I guess. Rothe's made it plain he won't let you use his road. He might put up a fight."

The listening men smiled, and Bloud grunted, "Him? Hell, I aim to wreck his toll station and kick his carcass down the gully. You object?"

"His wife will."

"Too bad," said Bloud. He glanced through the window at some of the roustabouts in the wagon yard.

Od caught the glance. He remembered the Duke's girl, beaten brutally, her jaw broken. That beating had been needless. Berry's case would be necessary and drastic. A wipe-out raid demanded a clean sweep, total elimination of hostile tale-bearers. That was what Bloud meant by doing it big. Bloud was entirely capable of pulling a Comanche play, burying the captive's broken body and afterward giving a plausible lie to account for the disappearance. Brutality was his sport.

Od shook his head, choking down a red rage. "I've told you before, this is not the border country! Don't you know Bowers is in town? I talked with him today. He doesn't like you. He's on watch!"

Puffing out his thick lips, Bloud said, "He's your problem! That's your job!"

"You're crazy!" Od rasped at him. "Pull this massacre, you'll be up before Judge Parker! You'll hang, and a few more with you!"

Bloud flung back his head, glaring, belligerent. A violent man, he hated dull waiting. He had no patience.

170

Frustration formed his lifelong enemy, to be smashed repeatedly, always to rise again.

Yet his eyes betrayed a grudging caution. This Texas Panhandle was not his country. He could not feel quite sure of himself here. Od's warning made him the more unsure, and so he looked for a guiding sign from Jim Kerry, who belonged nowhere and everywhere.

That silent man meditated for a while, watched intently by Bloud and the men. They respected his judgment and stood in some awe of him, partly because he carried reticence and impassiveness to such a cold-blooded extreme. He rubbed his nose with a thumb and shrugged slightly.

Bloud got out words as if strangling on them. "All right, we'll wait for Rothe's answer! It better be the right one! If it ain't — what then?"

Jim Kerry flattened out his right hand, palm downward, in a crushing gesture as clear in meaning as a speech.

Bloud nodded, sighing heavily. "We sure will, Jim — we sure as hell will!"

Od sighed, too, with relief. He had won only a delay, one last stall, yet with a ton of luck it might somehow be built up and made to postpone the disaster. He started to leave with his small victory, already speculating on how to use it, but then Ray Bowers walked into the Jims' office and his frigid smile told Od that Bowers brought disaster with him.

They faced each other at the office door. Bowers, eyes fixed on Od, said with dry politeness, "Excuse my intrusion, gentlemen. For my personal satisfaction I

171

wish to set you right about this man Thornton, your head partner! I've just learned from a certain person that this smooth-tongued faker is actually claiming to hold a pull over Judge —"

"Wait!" Od cut in. He stepped close to Bowers. He whispered urgently, "For God's sake, Bowers, snub it off! You don't know what you're doing! It's not only me!"

Shaking his head woodenly, Bowers raised a hand to Od's chest and pushed him back. "You've used me once too often! When you made a fool of me before Judge Parker, that was your time to quit and skin out of my territory! You've used me again. You've overplayed your hand!"

"Bowers — back me up this once and I'll give you any satisfaction you want!"

"Too late now," Bowers said, smiling, not lowering his voice. "Your luck has run out, Thornton! I'm here to beat your game and make a fool of you, as you did me! It's my whack!"

Bloud opened his mouth to roar a question at Bowers. Jim Kerry, rising, motioned him quiet and for once he spoke. "Thornton, turn around and let's see your face."

Od swung around. He had donned a poker mask, but after an instant's scrutiny Jim Kerry sent his pale glance ranging on to Bootjack Reid and the other men. Bootjack moved quietly, inserting himself between Od and the door.

Bowers bent his smile on Kerry. He stepped aside from the door, leaving Od standing alone. "You are

172

correct," he said. "Thornton has made fools of you, too! He four-flushed you, bluffed a head partnership out of you! Used you for suckers! You — the smart Jims! It'll be the big laugh of the Panhandle!"

His mouth widened and his face crinkled, although no sound of laughter came from him. "A pull with me and Parker? Him?" He pointed at Od. "I hate his guts! Parker's got him down on the book for next time!"

Od held his right hand low. He heard Bootjack Reid shift behind him, but couldn't spare a backward look because Bloud looked too ready.

Bowers said, "On top of it all, he's double-crossed you! Played both sides!" He pulled a crumpled and folded paper from his coat pocket. "This is addressed to the firm. For some reason of his own, which maybe you'll know, he held it out on you!"

Od dived his left hand at the message, recognizing it, but Bowers threw it to Bloud, who caught it nimbly.

Bloud unfolded the paper. He scanned the message, a single sentence written in pencil. "Rothe," he told Jim Kerry, "says we can't buy his road nor use it at any price. This is his answer to us. Sounds like he means it. Bone-head Dutchman!"

Bloud showed no excitement now, even his high color receding. He was as coolly self-possessed as he had been the night of the Little Red fiasco. He asked briskly, "Well, Jim?"

Jim Kerry nodded, but looked at Bowers.

Catching the look, Bowers said, "I'm leaving. I won't be back. I'm through." He stalked to the door, and Bootjack stood aside to let him pass.

173

Od followed closely behind Bowers. Bootjack palmed the butt of his holstered gun, and Od stopped.

One of the Jims must have sent a silent sign, for Bootjack let his hand fall. They would not shoot him down, Od felt, as long as Bowers was still on hand. Bowers wouldn't mind seeing Od dead, but he would also arrest the Jims for murder. And they knew it.

He fell in with Bowers outside and walked down the street with him in the blazing sunshine. "You've played hell!" he commented. Behind, at the Jims' office, he knew, they watched him, only waiting for Bowers to make good on his promise to leave town.

"I know," Bowers breathed softly, not smiling. "And you in the middle of it! I said I'd break you, didn't I?" His strange face quivered, the muscles jerking the dry skin into changing patterns. "Damn you, I said this was personal, didn't I?"

"You've done it," Od admitted. "But you've done for maybe a dozen others, too! The Jims will raid Rothe's road and catch Tolliver on it. It'll be a wipe-out! And there's Rothe's wife. She's on her way there. Bloud's been known to break a girl's jaw. His roustabouts are worse. Be proud of yourself, Bowers."

The cover of the Avalon was near at hand. Od talked for time.

Bowers, catching on, stopped short on the boardwalk. "Still using me, are you? I should've made it plainer to the Jims how through I am. Since the mail-stage went through, I'm not a United States marshal. I sent in my resignation. I'm leaving this damned country — and taking Gloria with me."

He stared at Od, and his right hand slid under his coat. It was obvious that he actually believed Od would fight to keep Gloria.

Od said, "I'll set up the champagne on that."

He entered the Avalon, turning his back on Bowers, who came in after him, eyes alive for Gloria and saying, "I'll make it plain to the Jims as soon as I get Gloria that I'm leaving and they can do what they want with you."

"Later on will do," Od said, but something in his voice evidently warned Bowers.

When Od whirled around, Bowers had his gun half out. Od smashed his right fist at Bowers's jaw and followed it fast with a left drive just below the chest. Bowers toppled backward, gasping. Od stroked out his gun and sledged him high above the eyes with the barrel.

The few customers jumped up. Od waved his gun and said, "A personal affair, friends." Gloria was not in the barroom.

To George, he called, "Go tell Ted to ready my horse and bring it to the back. Then you come to my room — I want a talk with you. Hurry, George!"

"Lord, that's Bowers you clouted!" George gulped. He had feared Od's growing soft streak. Now he feared Od's hard recklessness. He hurried to the front door, glancing at the downed Bowers. "You better set off on a long ride, Od, and keep on a-going!"

"Yes, George," Od said. He looked down at Bowers. "I know!"

He tore a velvet drape off a front window and bundled it under Bowers's senseless head. "It's been coming up for quite some time, this long ride."

"Oh, Lord!" groaned George, running out. He had known Od in wild moods in the past. This was the wildest yet. This Od was even tougher than the old Od.

CHAPTER
TEN

At Od's first glance the toll road appeared to hang by faith and a few sticks, high against the canyon wall. That was an illusion, however, tricked by distance and the clarity of the air at a mile above sea level.

In the narrow places where the road was bridged over with mountain pine and cottonwood logs, the red horse's hoofs clacked and boomed irregularly, the pitchy pine giving out one note, the cottonwood another. It bothered the horse and put it into a nervous fret.

Topping the last steep grade, Od came in sight of the toll station.

The old wagon stood near the door, not yet unloaded and the little Spanish mules still drooping in harness. Berry had safely reached home — if the sorry place could be called home.

Tolliver and Fabe Rothe walked around from a pen behind the toll station, Tolliver leading a saddled horse and apparently giving Rothe a tongue-lashing about something. They stopped short on seeing Od. Tolliver started a hand to his hip, but thought better of it when his eyes met Od's.

Rothe, less perceptive, came on, calling out, "My road's not open to you, Thornton. Turn back." With his fuzzy beard and shaggy hair Rothe could have passed for a crack-brained hermit, possibly dangerous.

Od swung down off his horse. "I'm a traveler passing through. How do you propose to stop me?" It was a bad beginning, though no worse than he had expected. If Rothe elected to fight, better to have it out at once and get through with it, quick. He hoped suddenly that Rothe would fight.

He watched Rothe halt and look back at Tolliver, and the angry hope waned. A man on the genuine scrap didn't stop to see who might back his play. Tolliver wasn't likely to chip in, not this minute.

Catching Rothe in uncertainty, Od said to spur him, "Last time we met I laid you out cold! Want me to do it again? If not, take your lousy dollar toll and tend to my horse! Make up your mind!"

Rothe shook his shaggy head. As if meeting challenge with challenge, he declared, "No! To you, the toll is five — it's ten dollars! And ten for the horse!"

Od led the red horse forward and held out the reins. "Rub him down before you water and feed him. A little grain, if you've got any. I'll be pushing on soon."

An hour, probably longer, was his estimate. He had wasted no time getting out of Trailtown. The Jims had nothing to match the fast red horse, and organizing their mob must have cost them some delay in getting started. The one snag lay in the possibility that Bootjack Reid's hard-riding squad might be racing ahead. That was a risk that had to be watched for and met if it came.

"If you aim to eat here," Rothe said sternly, "that'll be —"

"Ten more — to me, eh?" Od dug into a pocket. "Here's fifty, in case you think up any more little tariffs. Keep the change."

Rothe took the money and strode off like a victor with the red horse. Tolliver, his tone sarcastic, remarked to him that the two tired wagon-mules needed tending to, but Rothe led the horse on around to the pen without replying.

"Money sure talks around here!" Tolliver commented, gazing off. "It shouts louder'n the Gospel an' Griego's he-goat!"

"Yes," Od said, "it does. You should know."

Tolliver shrugged. "I do. I bought him, cheap. Well, you get what you pay for. But he owns this road, and I need it."

Od walked over to him. "Your second string of wagons have gone on, eh? They're on the road to Quemado. How long since they went through here? An hour?"

"More or less. Why?" Tolliver stood warily still, holding the reins of his saddled horse, suspicious of Od's curt questions.

"You better catch up and light a smart fire under your teamsters!" Od said. "It was a bad play, that, on the Mockingbird Hills!"

"So was the raid you and the Jims tried to pull on me at Little Red!" Tolliver retorted quickly. "I got off a shot at you, but it was dark and you was moving too fast!"

He stuck a thumb back at the butt poking from his saddle scabbard. "I carry a double-barrel shotgun since that night, loaded with buckshot!"

"It won't do you a lot of good," Od said. "The Jims are hot after you with a mob! They're not far behind me, I guess."

"Behind you? What's that mean?"

"I've split with the Jims. This is a one-way trip for me."

Tolliver dipped a glance at Od's waist. Od's open coat revealed two gunbelts, an unusual circumstance; it plainly signified trouble. And Od wore a preoccupied, distant expression, a look of listening. He was listening for the clack and boom of hoofs on the log bridges down along the road.

"I hate to believe you," Tolliver said. "This horse of mine is kinda lamed. Rothe tried to fix a loose shoe and made a botch of it. And charged me a dollar! But if you're right —"

"You better believe I'm right!"

Tolliver mounted his horse. "Well, maybe! Any rate, I'll feel more easy after I gather up the rest of my crew at Quemado. How about Rothe and his wife?" He ran his eyes disparagingly over the mule wagon. "That's one hell of a rig for a getaway! Your horse, though —"

Then, remembering gossip, he muttered, "You'd do well to get" — a jerk of his head toward the toll station — "*her* out! For more reasons than one!"

"It's on my mind," Od said.

Nodding, Tolliver said, "Rothe won't listen to you, of course. He won't leave here on your word. You'll have trouble, I expect."

"And you'll have trouble," Od told him, "if you're caught on the road with your wagons! It's getting late. When you catch up, I'd advise you and your teamsters to cut and run for Quemado!"

Tolliver laid a long look on him, and his face darkened an angry red. "That's the game, is it?" he said, twisting his mouth. "You damn near had me swallow your story! Abandon my loaded wagons on the road for you and the Jims, without a fight? The hell I will!"

He rode off abruptly on his limping horse, but soon reined to a walk and hipped around in the saddle to shout back, "You're the world's prize liar, Thornton, but you don't pull that trick on ol' Tolliver!"

After Tolliver departed, cursing him, Od walked into the toll station.

It was hard to fight off a deadening conviction of defeat, failure; the lives of others that he touched fell to pieces. Soft Duval, shot to death in a futile gunfight. The Duke broken past repair. Gloria had stooped to treachery. Ray Bowers, tempted into forgetting duty and rigid principles, had thrown away his career. And Berry . . .

Time pressed. Much of the hour was spent, to no profit. He still could not rush. Any urgent warning, from him, could arouse nothing here but skepticism, because here he was an enemy. Craft and clever guile

181

remained his only weapons, the truth having so little power in his hands.

He found Berry slumped on the bench nearest the kitchen door, her hands spread, palms up in her lap. His arrival up here was certainly known to her, as well as his dominant motive in coming. He was able to detect the defensive spirit in her waiting attitude. She still wore the cheap house dress that she had worn into Trailtown, and the sunbonnet hung behind her head by its tied strings.

She didn't look around, but she must have recognized his step, for she said dully, "Don't, Od! Please go away! I'm tired sick. And so much to do. Tolliver's men used the kitchen before I could get back. They cooked, slopped, wasted food. It's a mess!" She raised her head and laughed, a fluttering laugh that verged upon the despair of hysterics. "Everything is a mess! *I'm* a mess!"

He said reasonably, aiming for a normal note to steady her, "Oh, well — Tolliver's men are busy bees. I guess they didn't have time to clean up. Or they didn't even see the mess they made. You know how men are."

His aim scored a close miss, not quite close enough to prod up her battered sense of humor.

She laughed again in that mirthless way. "Men! The men who come through here never have time but to gobble food and rush on! Fabe's the same, though he doesn't have to rush on. I'm the cook, nothing more. Oh, God!" She put her hands up to her face. In such short time she had sunk to drudgery, unloved, unnoticed.

182

Shaken, Od stood waiting, hoping, not daring to speak, distrustful of breaking the strained dam of his emotions. A part of himself was gone to her for as long as he lived. He would never again be whole, without her. The sure knowledge of it made him humble and cautious.

At last Berry lowered her hands, saying, "You knew it would turn out this way. Didn't you? You timed it right! How did you know?"

He bowed his head. "I'm sorry. And glad. You don't belong here. And now you can't stay here. Will you come with me, Berry?"

She took her hands from her face and looked at him. "You want me, Od? Look at me! The way I am now?"

"The way you were," he told her gently. "The way you'll be again. But I want you even as you are."

He put his arms around her, drew her up off the bench, held her. Over her head he saw, through the open door, the massive slabs of bleak rock towering forbiddingly. He felt the shivering of her body in his arms.

She tried to push him away, saying, "No, Od! It's only because I happen to be one woman you didn't get. You have to keep trying, because you're what you are. And should you win —" She shrugged. "That's all!"

He let his arms drop. "You believe that?"

She gazed up at him, her eyes strangely kind, more than kind. "It's your way. I heard what Tolliver shouted at you. I'm afraid he's right, Od! Lies and trickery — you can't help it. Any woman would be mad who'd trust herself to you."

They heard Fabe Rothe approach, and stepped apart. Berry said, "Sit down, and I'll get your meal."

"I don't want anything, thanks. There isn't time."

"I saw you pay for it. For ten meals!"

Od managed a smile. "For the good of the cause."

Berry nodded. "Like the half-price groceries. Like the no-charge at the livery. And the Chinaman's lunch, roast chicken and wine. If only —" She caught herself. "Coffee and whisky?"

"If it's no bother to you," Od said. When she left him he sat staring down at the floor, thinking of what she had said.

Rothe, finished with Od's horse, set to work unloading the wagon of the supplies that Berry had bought in Trailtown. He lugged in each box, slammed it onto the table, and went through the contents, weighing every item in his hand and consulting the list.

During one of Rothe's trips out to the wagon Berry brought in the coffee and whisky, and Od said to her, "My time has run out in Trailtown. I'm going to California. George will sell the Avalon and join me in San Francisco. I'll get into a different kind of business out there. Be years, I think, before I'll want to come back to Texas."

"Then I — we won't be seeing each other again?"

Her reaction gave him, he considered, enough warrant to say carefully, "No. Unless, that is, you'll take a chance on San Francisco. It's a good town. Shows and theaters, even an opera house, I hear."

"Bribery," she murmured, unsmiling. "You know me so well, you think! But you don't. I'm married to Fabe.

184

I'll never run off like a cheap little welsher with some man who has taken a fancy to her legs!"

Fabe Rothe clumped in carrying another box, and went through the same examining process. That Berry's purchases in Trailtown were bargains there was no doubt, but the only remark Rothe made to her was that he hadn't had his dinner yet.

For an instant Berry's eyes flashed in the way that Od well remembered. But she went to the kitchen. Two people living alone in cramped quarters dared not risk a quarrel. She had learned that painful lesson.

Od suddenly thought of the Jims. During the last few minutes he had forgotten to listen for them. Rothe's noise made it impossible, anyway.

Rising, Od said to Rothe, "Forget that stuff! The Jims are coming on the prod! You and your wife jump on that wagon and get out of here!" Too abrupt, he knew, but clever guile had deserted him.

Rothe dropped a package and blinked at him. "What?"

Berry came to the kitchen door, her eyes pitying. Her lips silently formed the words, "Lies and trickery."

Aloud Berry said as if to a stubborn child, "No, Od, that won't do. Please go now."

"I'm in lawful possession here!" Rothe declared, wagging a hand at Od. "*You* get out!"

Here it was, the final failure. They might have believed him, Od supposed, had he not been who and what he was. He said, moving toward Rothe, "Bowers is out, and the law is a long way off from this godforsaken place. Get going, I tell you!"

Rothe backed off into the light of the open door.

Od measured the distance for a leap and a blow, but then he saw horsemen outside and knew it was too late.

Catching Od's raised stare, Rothe turned about and he, too, saw them: five quiet men.

Od said softly, "They're riders for the Jims, on scout! Watch out, Rothe! I know 'em! That first one is Bootjack Reid!" He cursed himself for having forgotten to listen, those minutes with Berry, when the hoofs must have banged on the bridges.

Rothe didn't know them. "Cowhands," he said, going out to collect his toll. He didn't know a cowhand from a gunman. He went by the clothes, not expression and manner.

Following Rothe with his eyes, Od said to Berry, "Call him back, quick!" He sensed the readiness of the five. They didn't bunch. They separated, each broadsiding his mount to hide a hand resting on a gun. "In a minute they'll shoot!"

Her laugh was tiredly skeptical. "You're a good actor, Od! You should have better lines!"

"Have it your way," he said, and shrugged. It wasn't possible to shed the weight of past mistakes. He eased over to a window. It was too late, anyhow, for Rothe to take cover. Rothe stood out there, unarmed, a dead duck for fair.

Bootjack Reid circled his horse to halt just beyond the mule wagon. The four other riders drew in at intervals, so that they sat spaced out, faces turned to the door. Their eyes, searching and meditative, played over Rothe. They had not yet spied the red horse in the little pen behind the toll station.

"One dollar each," Rothe announced. Because of their cool manner, he added with an attempt at geniality, "That's all I charge folks that look right to me! How about eating? My wife's cooking right now, and I'll make you a price."

Bootjack, lounging in his saddle, looked away and said, "Pay him, Breck."

Breck, a dull man, said unemotionally, "Me? All right." His right arm bent.

Od called, "Duck, Rothe!" — and as the five darted their eyes at the window he blasted it out with a shot, to shake Breck's draw.

After that, confusion swirled. Breck and Bootjack both fired together, though at different targets.

Od got Breck with his second shot, and tried for Bootjack, but all five horses were already in a rearing whirl and the startled mules sprang alive in the midst of it. The spin of his horse threw the swaying Breck; his right boot went through the stirrup and the horse dragged him when he fell.

Because Bootjack and his horse and flaming gun loomed in their way, the mules dodged hard over. They slung the careening wagon broadside at him. The horse jumped straight up, and Bootjack rose a foot higher and came down half out of the saddle.

Od took his aim off that dust-fogged tangle. He laid two shots at a rider who, drawn up, was punching bullets close to the window.

The rider slithered to earth and braced his gun on the saddle. Splinters flew from the window frame. Od ducked to the door and shot down that one.

The wagon capsized on the tight turn, the off wheel collapsing under the strain, strewing broken boards and seat and a sack of flour that burst like a silent white bomb. Bootjack Reid thundered past the front of the toll station, his gun flashing, and he kept right on going, for the other two were pulling out.

The two riderless horses bolted after them, one still dragging Breck, and the mules followed, the remnant of the wagon shedding pieces at every bounce.

Rothe lay face down in the dirt. Even before the riders vanished back down the toll road, Berry ran out to him, crying, "Fabe! Oh, God — he's hurt!"

Fabe Rothe was hurt, all right. Breck had faithfully paid him, on Bootjack's order. A bullet in his chest. Smart shot, all things considered. Helped by Berry, Od carried him inside the toll station.

While doing so, Od heard faint shouts far down the toll road, and a couple of echoing gun reports. Bootjack and the other two, he guessed, were having trouble with those runaway mules plunging after them down the narrow road with the wreck of the wagon in tow.

Rothe bled at the mouth, and Od said, "Got to get him down to Quemado to a doctor! Tolliver would help, if we catch up with his wagons."

He tried to reckon how long it should take for the Jims and their main force of roustabouts to reach here. Bootjack and the riders had come ahead on a fast scout, being engaged and paid for such special tasks;

188

the roustabouts were not in their class as horsemen, but they would provide the murderously massive power to wipe out opposition.

To his amazement, Berry turned on him fiercely, whispering, "You deliberately brought this on to get him killed, didn't you? You'll do anything to have your way! You forced those men into a fight, and killed two of them! You killer!"

She held a clean towel pressed against Rothe's wound. The bullet hole was small, not bleeding much, but she didn't know what else to do.

The bullet had got Rothe low and somewhat to the right. It had not come out through his back, and there was no way to tell which direction it might have ranged.

Rothe revived for a moment after they got him into the tiny bedroom. He opened his eyes and stretched out on the bed as if merely to rest a while. Then a change came over him, with memory and realization.

He whimpered, "I'm hurt. Do something!" And, as his eyes found Berry's face, "Get me a doctor! Get the law! They" — his eyelids dropped — "they didn't — pay me — no toll . . ."

Od reloaded his guns, spun their cylinders, holstered them. He wondered if, when wounded like Rothe, he would be able to raise his thoughts above profit and loss. His loss — Berry — would be on his mind to the last, yes; so he was in no shape to look down on Rothe, who happened to love cash.

Rothe said mutteringly, "Somebody coming up the road!" His senses were slipping away, sinking into delirium, and his eyes took on an anxious stare. He attempted to get up, to go out and collect toll. Berry pressed him back.

Od said, "I'll see to it." He left quickly, needing to get out of that tiny room, away from the stabbing condemnation of Berry's eyes and words and manner.

Outside, nothing moved. A slight sound caused him to whip a look at the two dead men before locating it. The sound, a scraping, followed by a rattle of stones, had come from somewhere down the road. He didn't hear it again, and guessed it had been the last kick of a dying mule. He walked around to the pen behind the toll station.

While saddling his horse he abruptly tensed in raging anguish, cursing, all his cool defenses smashed by the certain knowledge of what he was going to do. Along the line he had missed out and let himself in for this. He, who knew all the tricks. Beaten by a dollar-grubbing clod who lacked the brains to run a toll road as it should be run and stay out of trouble.

Good poker taught a man how to lose, he reflected, lighting a cigar. Men who had never gambled, never lost their last chip, were like men who had never been tempted to sin. In the pinch they generally had no tested strength to rely on, to see them through. Heaven, perhaps, instead of being the playground of unsullied souls, was the haven of rascals who had made it the hard way.

He heard that scraping sound again. Somebody or something moved fumblingly on the road, that was sure, but whether far or near he couldn't tell. He led the horse around to the front of the toll station and called through the door to Berry, "If Rothe catches up with Tolliver's outfit, he could ride in one of the wagons to Quemado. Tolliver would get him to a doctor there."

Berry came to the door. "I thought you were gone," she said.

It made him flinch, her obvious belief that since he couldn't win her, he would simply desert her and ride on. He could see her viewpoint. By his own actions, and by his reputation, he had contributed to it. Still, it hurt.

"No," he said quietly. His face felt cold, drenched with icy sweat. "I'm not gone. Rothe's going. On my horse."

"He can't ride — not in his condition! He couldn't stay on! You know it!"

He shrugged, feeling as he supposed Soft Duval had felt, old, walking forward into a hopeless shoot-out. "I know. You'll go with him, to hold him on."

The flare leaped into her eyes. "It would kill him! That's what you want!"

He puffed his cigar to a glow, listening — not to her but to the toll road. "He'll die if he stays here. The Jims are after him as well as Tolliver. Their mob will be drunk, this time of day. They'll drag Rothe out and boot him down the canyon! And what Bloud will do to you — ! Yes, he's going, you with him!"

"No!"

"Yes," he said. "We'll tie him on."

He didn't quite look at her. His eyes were far off with his listening ears. The Jims' mob was bound to come roaring up the road soon. They wouldn't creep and fumble, making that faint and furtive sound that he kept hearing.

"Get a blanket," he told Berry. "I've got a rope. You ride the blanket behind him and hold him up. Let's get busy, now! Or must I clout you and haul him out and rope on the pair of you?"

He was tough enough to do it. Right now he looked merciless, his eyes so remote, his face dispassionate.

"You killer! You —"

"Snub it!" he said. His glance touched on her for a bare instant, and shuttled off. "Let's get busy, I say — for the last time! You've got to go!"

By his forcing, they carried Rothe out of the toll station and hoisted him into the saddle. Od tied him on, with care and some gentleness. Rothe didn't look likely to survive much of a ride, but death in the saddle was preferable to a kicked roll down a canyon.

Od lifted Berry up behind Rothe, setting her spread-legged on the folded blanket. Berry clasped Rothe in her arms, Rothe sagging. Her fingers took the reins that Od put into them. Her eyes blazed.

"This is the worst thing you ever did, Od! You're betting this will kill him. But I'll beat you. And when you come to Quemado," she said, "I'll be waiting there for you — with a gun."

"That, Berry," he said, smiling, "I'll have to take my chances on."

He slapped the red horse and sent it on its way with its double load, and when he was alone he walked into the empty toll station.

He dragged the table to a window facing the last hump of the toll road. He smashed out the window with the poke of a gun. Unhurried, he thumbed shells from his belt-loops and arrayed them on the table, and placed his two guns there.

He pulled up a bench and sat down to wait, smoking his cigar, thinking of Berry. His recollections tracked back, pausing here and there for pleasure: the light in her eyes at the Chinaman's that evening; her hushed enchantment when he first guided her into the splendid palace car on the train. She was no pioneer woman, God knew, and a faded house dress and sunbonnet couldn't make her into one.

He remembered the tired settlers, with their battered wagons, that he and she saw from the window of the palace car, toiling south toward the lower Pecos Valley. Misled by the glowing report of some starry-eyed greenhorn who had skittered through that country during a rare spell of rain, they and others like them were unwittingly responsible for all this violence and disaster. They had seeded and nurtured the Quemado boom.

Tolliver and the Jims, too obsessed with their cutthroat contest to grab the trade, had not taken time out to recognize the Quemado boom as a flash in the pan. Nor Rothe, slaving on his toll road, intent upon creating for himself a secure prosperity.

Security was a mirage. Nothing lasted, except humanity and the ancient code — a few decent principles, a fair integrity. In the long run, nothing else was worth great struggle and strain and violence. Od

193

raised his musing eyes, catching a distinct sound of stumbling feet. He placed his cigar down on the table's edge and lifted a gun, watching for the oncoming walker to bulge up over the hump of the toll road.

It was Ray Bowers.

Hatless and afoot, dirty beyond the belief of anybody knowing his usual neatness, Bowers came up the road at a shambling trot. He fell twice, toppling full length, before reaching the toll station.

He floundered clumsily through the open door and caught a toe on the wooden step, sprawling in like a load of firewood delivered in a hurry. He pushed himself strenuously up onto his knees, peered at Od, and sent his right hand digging at the holster under his coat.

Besides the bruised gash on his forehead, made by Od's gunbarrel in the Avalon, one side of Bowers's face glistened blood-wet from fresh cuts and grazes. His clothes hung torn and smeared with dust and damp blotches. A dark stain spread over his white shirt-front.

He quit fumbling at his holster. It held no gun. "Must've lost it when the mules hit me," he said, rising wearily to his feet. "I never have luck with you, Thornton!"

"You came after me?" Od asked him.

Bowers lurched to the door. He slammed it shut and leaned against it. "They rode me down. Bootjack Reid and two others. At a sharp bend. Coming like hell. We met head-on. My horse went down the canyon. I swapped a shot or two after 'em. They fired back and got me. Then a coupla damn mules knocked me down again! Yeah — I came after you!"

"Glad of your company," Od said. He listened to sudden thunder far down the road — hoofs hammering on the bridges. "But I wish you had a gun."

Bowers, misunderstanding, wholly wrapped up in his own personal affairs, laughed harshly. "Doesn't matter now, I guess! You're caught tight here, Thornton, seems to me! You slipped up somewhere. The Jims are coming with their whole mob!"

"I hear them coming," Od said. "Pick yourself a window. I'll loan you a gun. Not more'n two-three can charge up over that hump at a time. I figure we can stand 'em off till dark."

"You, maybe," said Bowers. "Not me!"

Od sent him a searching look, and saw what he meant. Bowers couldn't keep his knees from buckling.

Bowers slid slowly down the door until he squatted. In the collision and gun-duel on the road, he had got the worst of it. He breathed noisily in the quiet cabin, like a sleeping man snoring. His shirt-front showed now no white at all, only a brownish red.

The clack and boom of hoofs striking the log bridges came louder, echoing up the canyon. Od took his look off Bowers and watched through the broken window.

Bowers let his head droop. He spat, and tried to wipe the bloody spittle from his mouth and only smeared it over his face. "Gloria wouldn't go with me," he said. "She turned me down. I guess she never really got over you, or trusted me."

"Tough," Od said. "I know how it is."

He sighted two hats topping the final hump of the toll road. They ducked when he fired, and held back, but the pressure of the mob proved too much. Bloud's voice rang out above the shouting babble, and the two hats bobbed up again, becoming two riders plunging into full view.

Od fired at the tallest one, Bootjack Reid. At this range, with the table for rest, he could hit a playing card.

Bootjack, forced by his position and his gun prestige into heading the rush, took Od's bullet high in the chest. His long, lean body jolted in the saddle, stiff as a stick, toppling backward. His drag on the reins spun the horse around, throwing him. Od's next shot clipped the other rider, who bowed low and swung back in a slither of dust and gravel. That put a cautious halt on the mob.

Bowers mumbled, "Where's that Dutchman — the toll keeper — and his wife?"

Od said, "They're gone. He got hurt. I sent 'em off. She'll be all right." He smiled, eyes on the hump. "All my money's on that red horse, stuffed in the saddle pockets. Yes, she'll be all right!"

Another hat bobbed up. He aimed a shot and sent it spinning, and for a moment he had peace.

"It's crazy, all this," he said to Bowers. "In a year or two those Pecos settlers will pull out. That country's not much good for farming, you know that. It'll be empty again. The army will abandon those new forts. Quemado — hell, it'll be gone and forgotten, like this toll road. The railroad will come down the Panhandle, sooner or later. Then good-bye to Trailtown, too!"

He could see it. Heze Johns, if he hung on, as most likely he would, some day would attain his ambition. Heze would be mayor — of a crumbling ghost town.

"I don't think I want to see that day," Od said.

Bowers muttered, chin on chest, "You won't!"

Od punched out empty shells and reloaded the acrid-smelling cylinders. Thinking of Berry, he said, "She likes grand opera, all that kind of stuff. Well, hell, it takes all kinds, eh?"

"You're good as dead, anyhow," Bowers whispered.

Three riders, clumsy horsemen, reared up, full of drunken courage. Shooting carefully, Od spilled two of them. He missed the third on account of his own gunsmoke, and that rider whirled back, sawing rein and bridle-bit as if driving a plow-mule.

Blowing away the smoke, Od said softly, "Sure — I should've told her I loved her, way back at the start. Funny how you never say what you mean — I mean to a woman — till you're in bed with her — and not always then. You know what I mean."

Bowers said nothing to that.

Od sighted two accurate shots at two more oncoming riders, one of them Bloud. He watched their horses pitch and buck around, empty-saddled. He watched Bloud crawl back to cover, and he refrained from putting another bullet into the wounded man.

While waiting for the next comers he said, "A damned poor business, this holding down a toll road, don't you reckon, Bowers? No future in it!"

Bowers said nothing. He was dead.

★　★　★

Tolliver called a halt shortly after sundown. His horse limped badly, and he muttered curses on Rothe for having pounded in a long nail clumsily to tighten the loose shoe. The lumbering great wagons came to a stop, wheels grinding and the teamsters bellowing profanely at the big Missouri mules.

In the comparative silence following the halt, Tolliver picked up the sound of a rider coming from behind. He was unsaddling his lamed horse when he heard it, and he dumped the saddle fast and slid the shotgun from its scabbard, growling a warning to the teamsters.

The road here ran windingly through black pine and scrub oak. Tolliver flattened against a wagon and raised the shotgun ready. His teamsters, armed with Winchester repeaters bought by him, took up positions here and there, for once keeping their mouths shut.

The oncoming horse paced into view at a brisk walk. At first, in the fading light, it appeared to carry a queerly shapeless rider. Tolliver hailed, "Who is it? Speak up!"

"Help me!" came the response, and he recognized the voice of Rothe's young wife. "My husband is hurt!"

Tolliver stood the shotgun against the wagon and walked up the road and met the red horse. "Well!" he said. "All right, let go — I'll hold him on."

Fabe Rothe, tied into the saddle, couldn't fall off. But the upper part of his body lolled limply forward and would have dangled over without Berry's holding hands.

At the wagons, Tolliver helped Berry off the horse and kept an arm out for her to cling to. Her muscles, strained and cramped, would have let her fall as soon as her feet touched the ground. He made her sit down, her back against the wagon wheel where he had stood ready. She didn't speak.

The teamsters untied Rothe and lowered him to the ground. They lit lanterns and a fire, and carried Rothe to the light to see what could be done for him. Tolliver went over to them.

Soon, he came back to Berry with a tin cup. "Whisky and water," he said, handing it to her. "Sorry we ain't got nothing better."

He sat on his heels, facing her. "Drink it. You need it. Thornton shot him, eh?"

Her parched throat constricted and she choked on the whisky, which Tolliver hadn't watered down much. "No," she answered when she regained her breath. "That would at least have been straightforward."

"Then how — ?"

"Od Thornton deliberately forced a fight on five men who rode up to the toll station. He fired on them from a window, while Fabe was outside talking with them. It was the kind of murderous trick that only a madman would do! He killed two of those men, to get Fabe shot!"

"Sounds wrong. He must've been drunk." Tolliver twisted his head to look wonderingly at the red horse. "And got himself shot, too, eh?"

"No. He tied Fabe on, and made me —"

"What?" Tolliver brought his face around, astonished. "Are you telling me he gave you his horse and left himself afoot? He sure *is* crazy! Why, that's — Hey, wait a minute! Who were those jiggers he smoked it out with?"

Berry shook her head. "I never saw them before, as far as I know. He pretended they were gunmen, come to attack the toll station, but even I could tell they were just cowhands. I think he said one of them was called Bootjack, something like that."

Tolliver gave a start. "Tall feller? Thin? Quiet-spoken, like?"

"Yes. They were all five quiet, well-behaved men, until —"

"Bootjack Reid!" Tolliver said. He shot to his feet. "By God, Thornton told the truth!"

Berry raised her head. "What do you mean?"

"I mean," Tolliver snapped, "they were gunmen. Riders for the Jims. Bootjack Reid's their top trigger. And Thornton smoked 'em off, eh? Son of a — ! We got to cut and run, like he said, and leave the wagons! You climb back on that horse and hit for Quemado, right now and *muy pronto!*"

"But —"

"Look, I got no time to get in any argument! The Jims are after me, understand? Bootjack and his ladinos, hell, they ain't all! Thornton said the whole mob's coming! Maybe he's crazy — looks like it — but not on that, I'd say now, though I did call him a liar."

"So did I. My husband —"

"Little lady," said Tolliver, almost gently, "Rothe's dead. That's what I came to break to you. The boys couldn't do a thing for him."

He waved an arm to express to her his urgency. "Thornton's all that stands between us and the Jims' mob, and by this time he's dead, too, I bet — or soon will be! He can't stand off forty, maybe more, in the dark. He's gone plain gun-crazy! Fell out with the Jims, and bound and bedamned for a shoot-out! I knew he'd come to it soon'r later!"

She sat on the ground, looking up at him, her back pressed against the wagon wheel and her elbow nudging the shotgun that he had stood beside it. Her eyes grew enormous and blazingly alive in the deepening dusk. She did not have the stricken and crushed look that Tolliver expected of a suddenly bereaved young widow.

Tolliver had feared that crushed look, and impatiently prepared himself to meet it and the invariable burst of forlorn and hysterical sobbing. He'd knocked around in his time and had had this sad-news-breaking task to do on other occasions. He wasn't a heartless man; once or twice, when the dead man had been extra-valuable to him, he had even left some money with the family, to tide them over long enough for him to forget about them.

It disturbed him that this young widow behaved contrary to pattern. She didn't sob, didn't look forlorn or crushed. She looked angry — and Tolliver suspected that he stood as one of the objects of her wrath. It dawned on him that she had struck him from the first as an odd number, a queer one, potentially as moonstruck as that crazy Thornton, who threw away his last chance and elected to make a mad stand against forty or more desperate men.

Berry rose, saying strangely, "You're a fool! You're as big a fool as I am! I told him I'd be mad to trust him. I called him a killer. He's up there alone — he *knew* they were coming — and he smiled at me. He smiled when he sent me off!"

Tolliver took no time to untangle any of that except the statement that he was a fool, which he didn't accept. "You climb on that horse," he told her again. "We got to skin out in a hurry! Those Jims and their mob, if they catch us —"

"Yes," Berry said, hurrying to the horse. She tucked up her skirt and straddled the saddle, man-style. It was a lot of horse and saddle, for her size.

"Hey — you got my shotgun!" Tolliver yelled, and lunged after her. He had paid a good price for it.

"Yes!" Berry said, reining around to leave. Tolliver reached for the bridle. She brought the shotgun over, striking wildly in wordless impatience at his arm.

She had used a shotgun before, back home, but never as a club. Unwieldy to her hand, the heavy double barrel missed the horse's cheek by a hair. Tolliver had hung a tobacco sack of spare shells to the trigger guard, for emergencies, and the sack flipped around and whacked her smartly on the knuckles like a schoolmaster's rebuking cane, almost causing her to drop the gun.

The red horse shied. Its powerful endurance was blunted some, but the near-swipe convinced it that this bit of a rider wasn't taking any nonsense. It took off on

202

a clattering run, hoofing showers of gravel, and Berry rode back up the road.

Tolliver, after he jumped clear, hugged his hurting forearm. To his staring teamsters he snarled, "In this godforsaken country *everybody* goes crazy soon'r later! Let's get out o' here!"

Clinging to the shotgun and the saddle-horn, Berry kept seeing Od's smile. The smile made everything clear now. He had two sides, yes — or two layers, rather — to his nature: the first a sandy topsoil, unstable, stirred by the winds of passion, violence, reckless self-indulgence. The second, just beneath, was rock. He was simply a man, human, therefore flawed and imperfect, humanly dangerous. The tiger belonged to nightmare.

Unashamedly, she wiped Fabe Rothe from her mind. As though Od were scanning her with those half-mocking eyes of his, she tried to smile back, but couldn't manage it.

She was too bodily sore, sliding and bumping on this hard saddle. Soft and unused parts smarted horribly, hot as fire, the skin rubbed broken. The stirrups were let out for a long-legged man and her toes failed to reach them. Her blistered and broken seat took solidly every bump, and she wasn't at all sure of staying on the running horse. She was positive she couldn't if the horse took a whim to shake her off.

With the closing of darkness Od estimated by minutes his remaining margin of time. Some of Bloud's men were already crawling up over the last hump of the toll road to close in on him, while others blazed out a constant firing to cover them. He caught fleeting glimpses of the creeping advance, but he could not afford any longer to spatter shots at shadows. His shells were down to a total of five, in one gun, the other gun discarded on the floor, empty.

The east windows of the toll station, shot ragged, allowed sight of a sliver of moon and a million stars in the blue-black sky. Furrowed like a miniature field erratically plowed, the table top was crisscrossed with splintered grooves. Four hours was a long time.

Od spent one shell on a flitting shadow, to delay the rest a bit longer. The shadow, thick and definitely a man, foreshortened to a shapeless lump, calling out calmly, "He got me, Jim!"

Od said, "I guess I got Bloud that time. Sounded like him."

He spoke to Ray Bowers, although aware that Bowers couldn't hear him. A dead acquaintance, though, was better than nobody, in this lonely jackpot. The place rasped his nerves, with its overhanging cliffs of black rock. He felt glad that Berry was well out of it. How she had stood it, with only that bonehead for company, that Rothe, he couldn't imagine. It would take a lot of laughter to beat off the forbidding bleakness of this cursed place, and nobody had ever known Rothe to laugh at any time.

"She's in the clear, anyway, even if I'm not," he said, stooping under the table to fish for his last cigar butt. A rifle cracked along the road, and the bullet clipped the table and smacked into the wall opposite. "I sure am not!"

The rifle, or another, sounded off three more times. A ricochet droned off the front of the toll station. Some marksman had worked forward to where he could spot the front in the pale light of the stars and slice of moon, and was sighting on the door, to make double certain of blocking any forlorn attempt at a run-out. One of Bootjack's pals, Od guessed; or maybe Jim Kerry, rumored to be a crack shot when he set his hand to it.

He shifted position and said, "Well, we can't die more'n once, can we, Bowers?"

He had thought he was reconciled to dying here, resigned to this finality, prepared for it. But he hated death, and never hated it more than now.

This life stacked up pretty good if you met it right and didn't try to crowd in the top cards on every deal. It would do fine until a better one came along. He reckoned he had pulled some of the worst damned boners a man of his years could pull and walk away from in health. He wished he could backtrack and straighten them out for all concerned. Especially Berry; her life had suffered badly from his touch. She would, he hoped, be able to go back and start over, with better luck the next time.

The rifle marksman kept firing, edging in gradually closer and spacing his shots — a pause to reload, and once more the unhurried pattern, one for the window and a couple for the door, back and forth. Others, encouraged, crept forward. Od gave up trying to keep track of them. Their muzzle flashes starred the dark road like a colony of lightning bugs swarming over a bog.

He thought he heard a running horse, west, behind him, but the night blared a racket of noises and freak echoes that bounced from cliff to cliff, and when he listened for it the sound broke off. The narrow mountain pass magnified every report and multiplied it. He could hardly tell whether six or sixty shooters crept at him.

A gun roared somewhere behind him, louder than the rifles. Its echoes boomed through the pass and died away down the canyon like distant thunder. He considered the chance that one of the Jims' crew had somehow slipped past the toll station, or had outdone a mountain goat and climbed by high over the cliffs. All the rifles fell silent, except the methodical one — a shot for the wrecked and gaping window, two at the door, over and over again. That shooter meant business, and was not to be diverted from it.

The loud gun roared again. This time, in the comparative quiet, Od heard the gun's whistling discharge and the sharp spit of buckshot striking the hard surface of the road.

A man cried out, and the relentless rifle at last quit. The creeping shadows broke and scattered, darting back. Od whipped a shot at one and brought it down.

The shotgun boomed twice, a fast one-two with hardly a pause between, such as an excited gunner might commit, squeezing both triggers, or letting the kick of the first heavy discharge trigger off the second barrel.

"Od!"

The cry wailed down from some high point and he refused to believe it. He crouched at the window, waiting. A nighthawk might utter such a call, soaring over the pass, and imagination could do the rest. More likely it was a trick to entice him out and set him up for a quick shot. They were as tired of this stand-off as he was, he supposed. They didn't know he was spent and shaking from the long strain, down to three shells, and that a rush would finish him.

The shotgun repeated, both barrels as before, spraying the emptying road with a double blast of buckshot.

"Od!"

It had the sound of Berry's voice, though changed to a tone Od had never heard from her before. He hauled Bowers's body clear of the door and wrenched the door open. Incredulous, he shouted the first suspicious challenge that occurred to him. "Central City!"

"Victoria Hall!" came the response in an urgent scream.

"*Romeo et Juliette* — all seats one dollar — last and final — Od, come here, quick!" She sounded panicky. "Come here and help me!"

He burst out of the toll station. Firing had ceased, and back below the hump of the road a many-voiced argument loudly raged among the Jims' men, some of the unhurt pressing for a rush, others declaring against facing shotguns. But as soon as Od emerged blackly into the pale light, a lone rifle on the road spat at him.

The first bullet burned his neck. The next one, lower, snapped for his heart, punched his left shoulder below the bone. He knew that the third would get him, and he spun around and fired. The third missed him, and he turned and ran on and in a dozen steps he plunged into shadows.

The rifle rapped twice more, spearing blindly for him, then paused for the reloading. A severely determined shooter, that one. Probably Jim Kerry. He would come on, without hurry or fuss, regardless of what the arguing men decided. Od ran on, keeping to the shadows of the overhanging cliffs.

On a smooth patch of rocky floor, past the mule pen, he found his horse, ground-reined. The red horse threw up its head, sniffing, ears flat, anxiously disturbed. "Okay, Red, take it easy!" Od said, and had to take time to let the horse get his smell.

"Berry!" he called into the darkness. "Berry, where —"

"Come and help me!"

She had clambered over broken boulders of talus rock and part way up the cliff. Thanks to her familiarity with the mountain pass and its contours, she had recognized the need to reach a spot from which the shotgun could sweep the road, and she had got there.

Getting down again posed a different problem. She hung to a knob of rock, dangling above a sheer wall, her toes vainly searching for support and the shotgun lying below.

Od scrambled up the talus rock and got beneath her. "Let go, Berry!" he called up to her. "I'll catch you!"

She let go immediately and down she dropped, skirt fluttering. Od, standing braced, caught her. He had forgotten the wound in his left shoulder; the muscles cramped and twisted, burning as if stabbed with red-hot wires, but he made do to swing her clear of a jagged rock-edge and set her on her feet.

She stooped, snatching up the shotgun. They climbed down off the jumble of rocks and ran toward the horse. Remembering the red horse's nervous mood, Od slowed and said to Berry, "Easy now! Let's not spook ol' Red."

Obedient, Berry walked quietly beside him. The horse raised its head, snorting softly, and backed half around. It snorted again, louder, but not in their direction. Something troubled it.

Od said, "Go ahead. I'll be along presently."

Pacing away from Berry, he concentrated his attention on the short section of road between this spot and the bend at the empty mule pen. He tried to see into the shadows, to catch the first movement of the man who waited there for a sure shot. The horse knew that somebody stood there, near enough to smell him.

His nerves tightened and to his straining eyes all shadows twitched. A half-dozen places tempted him to shoot. He reminded himself that Jim Kerry, if it was he, must also be nerve-strung. Kerry had set himself the task of watching the horse, waiting for the rider to mount, and spilling him with a shot in the back. It made an upset in Kerry's calculations for the proposed target to come stalking him.

Od moved on, a slow step at a time, his drawn gun cocked and ready. One of those half-dozen deeper blobs of shadow was Kerry, motionless. Kerry could see him, no doubt of that. Kerry couldn't make a move without betraying himself; yet he would have to make that move, if only to level his rifle, any instant now.

All the shadows twitched again. They could all have been men in movement. Od forced himself to glance up at the stars, to relieve the strain on his eyes by lengthening their focus. A mad urge came to run forward and force Kerry's hand. He quelled it. A running man couldn't help but shoot wild. Cold patience was what won. This was a test of nerves, his against Kerry's, and damned if he'd crack before Kerry did.

He heard the click of a cocked hammer, followed by a dry snap, a lean sound, loud in the silence. It was behind him, and it took him a second or two to realize that it was the shotgun. Berry had triggered that piece, forgetting that she hadn't reloaded since her last double blast from up the cliff.

But it moved Jim Kerry. A shadow took on the shape of a man and a rising rifle. Od fired. The rifle flashed and Od felt the sweatband of his hat slip up and back out of place. He knew that he had hit Kerry and knocked his shot high.

Jim Kerry came on at a trudging half-trot, rifle lowered to waist-level, not uttering a sound. When within a distance of fifty feet he loosed another shot. His pale eyes were as calm as ever, but his mouth had twisted out of its straight line. He fired wild.

Od took aim at him, and hesitated on the trigger-squeeze. The man was hurt, staggering. But the bolt clicked in the breech and the rifle-muzzle veered at him. He tripped the hammer and got Kerry once more.

Kerry reeled aside, the rifle drooping, and gasped. The rifle spurted into the ground, exploding a tiny shower of dirt. Jim Kerry fell on the rifle and lay still except for his straightening legs, boots slowly scraping on the road.

Od turned and walked back to the stretch of floor-rock, where Berry stood holding the reins of the horse. He took the reins from Berry and swung up into the saddle and gave her a hand to scramble up behind him. He kicked the horse on and settled its gait to a rocking lope. His every action bore the stamp of unemotional efficiency.

A mile down the mountain road he pulled the horse to a halt, and was sick. Noisily and revealingly sick at his stomach.

"It's no good!" he said, wiping his mouth wretchedly. "No good!"

"What's no good?" Berry asked, hanging on behind him.

He dropped his sodden handkerchief. "Me, for one thing. Old George could tell you. He knows about me. I'm a has-been."

"So am I. Maybe it's age creeping up on us." She kept her arms around his waist, although the horse was at rest. And she laughed a little at the thought of age, for she was young, a girl again, warm and in bloom.

"Od, why did you stay behind?"

Od said, "What else could I do? They were all for a shoot-out, weren't they? If the bastards had got hold of you — Oh, hell! All right, I'll get you back to New York or Minnesota or wherever you say!"

The tiring red horse nosed some scant grass, and snuffed disgustedly, wanting grain and fresh water and the spoiling attentions of Ted Sieker.

Berry asked Od, "Why?" to his promise.

It posed the kind of feminine question that could exasperate any man. Od said, "Because that's where you belong, don't you? I'm shipping you home."

Berry seemed to revolve that in her mind. Then she asked him, "Od, do you love me?" At that moment she discovered the blood-wet spread beneath his left shoulder, and she drew in a quick breath. Od had not mentioned the wound.

"Dammit to hell!" Od exploded. "Girl, if you don't know that by now you never will!"

He felt her rubbing her forehead against his back, while he lifted the reins and urged the red horse on along toward Quemado. He heard her say, "Darling — I guess I know! Darling, please don't send me home, will you? Please let me stay with you wherever you go!"

Then he jerked up the reins and turned around to her, right-side, his right arm reaching wide over in the dark. He pulled her to him and found that her face was wet against his, her eyes blinded by tears. But she laughed as he kissed her, a choking laugh deep in her throat, her mouth pressing fully against his.